George Mac Donald

David Elginbrod

In three volumes. Vol. 3

SALZWASSER
VERLAG

George Mac Donald

David Elginbrod

In three volumes. Vol. 3

Reprint of the original, first published in 1863.

1st Edition 2022 | ISBN: 978-3-37500-633-4

Verlag (Publisher): Salzwasser Verlag GmbH, Zeilweg 44, 60439 Frankfurt, Deutschland
Vertretungsberechtigt (Authorized to represent): E. Roepke, Zeilweg 44, 60439 Frankfurt, Deutschland
Druck (Print): Books on Demand GmbH, In de Tarpen 42, 22848 Norderstedt, Deutschland

DAVID ELGINBROD

VOL. III.

DAVID ELGINBROD

BY

GEORGE MAC DONALD M.A.

AUTHOR OF

"WITHIN AND WITHOUT," "PHANTASTES,"

&c.

"And gladly wolde he lerne and gladly teche."

IN THREE VOLUMES

VOL. III.

LONDON:

1863.

CONTENTS OF VOL. III.

BOOK II.

CONTINUED.

ARNSTEAD.

BOOK III.

LONDON.

BOOK II.

CONTINUED.

ARNSTEAD.

> The earth hath bubbles as the water has.
>
> MACBETH.—I. 3.

DAVID ELGINBROD.

CHAPTER XXIX.

HUGH'S AWAKING.

But ah! believe me, there is more than so,
That works such wonders in the minds of men;
I, that have often proved, too well it know;
And whoso list the like assays to ken,
Shall find by trial, and confess it then,
That beauty is not, as fond men misdeem,
An outward shew of things that only seem!

. . . .

But ye, fair dames, the world's dear ornaments,
And lively images of heaven's light,
Let not your beams with such disparagements
Be dimmed, and your bright glory darkened quite;
But, mindful still of your first country's sight,

> Do still preserve your first informed grace,
> Whose shadow yet shines in your beauteous face.
>
> SPENSER.—*Hymn in Honour of Beauty.*

WHEN Hugh came to himself, he was lying, in the first grey of the dawn, amidst the dews and vapours of the morning woods. He rose and looked around him. The Ghost's Walk lay in long silence before him. Here and there a little bird moved and peeped. The glory of a new day was climbing up the eastern coast of heaven. It would be a day of late summer, crowned with flame, and throbbing with ripening life. But for him the spirit was gone out of the world, and it was nought but a mass of blind, heartless forces.

Possibly, had he overheard the conversation, the motions only of which he had overseen the preceding night, he would, although equally perplexed, have thought more gently of Euphra; but, in the mood into which even then he must have been thrown, his deeper feelings towards her could hardly have been different from what they were now. Although he had often felt that Euphra was not very good, not a suspicion had crossed his mind as to what he would have called the *purity* of her nature. Like many youths, even of character inferior to his own, he had the loftiest notions of feminine grace, and unspottedness in thought and feeling, not to say action and aim. Now he found that he had loved a woman who would creep from her chamber, at the cost of great suffering, and almost at the risk of her life, to meet, in the night and the woods, a man no better than an assassin—probably a thief. Had he been more versed in the ways of women, or in the probabilities of things, he would have judged that the very extravagance of the action demanded a deeper explanation than what seemed to lie on the surface. Yet, although he judged Euphra very hardly upon those grounds, would he have judged her differently had he actually known all? About this I am left to conjecture alone.

But the effect on Hugh was different from what the ordinary reader of human nature might anticipate. Instead of being torn in pieces by storms of jealousy, all the summer growths of his love were chilled by an absolute frost of death. A kind of annihilation sank upon the image of Euphra. There had been no such Euphra. She had been but a creation of his own brain. It was not so much that he ceased to love, as that the being beloved—not died, but—ceased to exist. There were moments in which he seemed to love her still with a wild outcry of passion; but the frenzy soon vanished in the selfish feeling of his own loss. His love was not a high one—not such as thine, my Falconer. Thine was love indeed; though its tale is too good to tell, simply because it is too good to be believed; and we do men a wrong sometimes when we tell them more than they can receive.

Thought, Speculation, Suggestion, crowded upon each other, till at length his mind sank passive, and served only as the lists in which the antagonist thoughts fought a confused battle without herald or umpire.

But it is amazing to think how soon he began

to look back upon his former fascination with a kind of wondering unbelief. This bespoke the strength of Hugh's ideal sense, as well as the weakness of his actual love. He could hardly even recall the feelings with which, on some well-remembered occasion, he had regarded her, and which then it had seemed impossible he should ever forget. Had he discovered the cloven foot of a demon under those trailing garments—he could hardly have ceased to love her more suddenly or entirely. But there is an aching that is worse to bear than pain.

I trust my reader will not judge very hardly of Hugh, because of the change which had thus suddenly passed upon his feelings. He felt now just as he had felt on waking in the morning and finding that he had been in love with a dream-lady all the night: it had been very delightful, and it was sad that it was all gone, and could come back no more. But the wonder to me is, not that some loves will not stand the test of absence, but that, their nature being what it is, they should outlast one week of familiar intercourse.

He mourned bitterly over the loss of those feelings, for they had been precious to him. But could he help it? Indeed he could not; for his love had been fascination; and the fascination having ceased, the love was gone.

I believe some of my readers will not need this apology for Hugh; but will rather admire the facility with which he rose above a misplaced passion, and dismissed its object. So do not I. It came of his having never *loved*. Had he really loved Euphra, herself, her own self, the living woman who looked at him out of those eyes, out of that face, such pity would have blended with the love as would have made it greater, and permitted no indignation to overwhelm it. As it was, he was utterly passive and helpless in the matter. The fault lay in the original weakness that submitted to be so fascinated; that gave in to it, notwithstanding the vague expostulations of his better nature, and the consciousness that he was neglecting his duty to Harry, in order to please Euphra and enjoy her society. Had he persisted in doing his duty, it would at least have kept his mind more healthy, lessened the absorption of his passion, and given him opportunities of reflection, and moments of true perception as to what he was about. But now the spell was broken at once, and the poor girl had lost a worshipper. The golden image with the feet of clay might arise in a prophet's dream, but it could never abide in such a lover's. Her glance was powerless now. Alas, for the withering of such a dream! Perhaps she deserved nothing else; but our deserts, when we get them, are sad enough sometimes.

All that day he walked as in a dream of loss. As for the person whom he had used to call Euphra, she was removed to a vast distance from him. An absolutely impassable gulf lay between them.

She sent for him. He went to her filled with a sense of insensibility. She was much worse, and suffering great pain. Hugh saw at once that she knew that all was over between them, and that he had seen her pass his door, or had been in her room, for he had left her door a little open, and she had left it shut. One pathetic, most pitiful glance of deprecating entreaty she fixed upon him, as after a few moments of speechless waiting, he turned to leave the room—which would have remained deathless in his heart, but that he interpreted it to mean: "Don't tell;" so he got rid of it at once by the grant of its supposed request. She made no effort to detain him. She turned her face away, and, hard-hearted, he heard her sob, not as if her heart would break—that is little—but like an immortal woman in immortal agony, and he did not turn to comfort her. Perhaps it was better—how could he comfort her? Some kinds of comfort—the only kinds which poor mortals sometimes have to give—are like the food on which the patient and the disease live together; and some griefs are soonest got rid of by letting them burn out. All the fire-engines in creation can only prolong the time, and increase the sense of burning. There is but one cure: the fellow-feeling of the human God, which converts the agony itself into the creative fire of a higher life.

As for Von Funkelstein, Hugh comforted himself with the conviction that they were destined to meet again.

The day went on, as days will go, unstayed, unhastened by the human souls, through which they glide silent and awful. After such lessons as he was able to get through with Harry,—who, feeling that his tutor did not want him, left the room as soon as they were over—he threw himself on the couch, and tried to think. But think he could not. Thoughts passed through him, but he did not think them. He was powerless in regard to them. They came and went of their own will: he could neither say *come* nor *go*. Tired at length of the couch, he got up and paced about the room for hours. When he came to himself a little, he found that the sun was nearly setting. Through the top of a beech-tree taller than the rest, it sent a golden light, full of the floating shadows of leaves and branches, upon the wall of his room. But there was no beauty for him in the going down of the sun; no glory in the golden light; no message from dream-land in the flitting and blending and parting, the constantly dissolving yet ever remaining play of the lovely and wonderful shadow-leaves. The sun sank below the beech-top, and was hidden behind a cloud of green leaves, thick as the wood was deep. A grey light instead of a golden filled the room. The change had no interest for him. The pain of a lost passion tormented him—the aching that came of the falling together of the ethereal walls of his soul, about the space where there had been and where there was no longer a world.

A young bird flew against the window, and fluttered its wings two or three times, vainly seeking to overcome the unseen obstacle which the glass presented to its flight. Hugh started and shuddered. Then first he knew, in the influence of the signs of the approaching darkness, how much his nerves had suffered from the change that had passed. He took refuge with Harry. His pupil was now to be his consoler; who in his turn would fare henceforth the better, for the decay of Hugh's pleasures. The poor boy was filled with delight at having his big brother all to himself again; and worked harder than ever to make the best of his privileges. For Hugh, it was wonderful how soon his peace of mind began to return after he gave himself to his duty, and how soon the clouds of disappointment descended below the far horizon, leaving the air clear above and around. Painful thoughts about Euphra would still present themselves; but instead of becoming more gentle and sorrowful as the days went on, they grew more and more severe and unjust and angry. He even entertained doubts whether she did not know all about the theft of both rings, for to her only had he discovered the secret place in the old desk. If she was capable of what he believed, why should she not be capable of *anything* else? It seemed to him most simple and credible. An impure woman might just as well be a thief too.—I am only describing Hugh's feelings.

But along with these feelings and thoughts, of mingled good and bad, came one feeling which he needed more than any—*repentance.* Seated alone upon a fallen tree one day, the face of poor Harry came back to him, as he saw it first, poring over *Polexander* in the library; and, full of the joy of life himself, notwithstanding his past troubles, strong as a sunrise, and hopeful as a Prometheus, the quivering perplexity of that sickly little face smote him with a pang. "What might I not have done for the boy! He, too, was in the hands of the enchantress, and, instead of freeing him, I became her slave to enchain him further." Yet, even in this, he did Euphra injustice; for he had come to the conclusion that she had laid her plans with the intention of keeping the boy a dwarf, by giving him only food for babes, and not good food either, withholding from him every stimulus to mental digestion and consequent hunger; and that she had objects of her own in doing so—one perhaps, to keep herself necessary to the boy as she was to the father, and so secure the future. But poor Euphra's own nature and true education had been sadly neglected. A fine knowledge of music and Italian, and the developement of a sensuous sympathy with nature, could hardly be called education. It was not certainly such a developement of her own nature as would enable her to sympathize with the necessities of a boy's nature. Perhaps the worst that could justly be said of her behaviour to Harry was, that, with a strong inclination to despotism, and some feeling of loneliness, she had exercised the one upon him in order to alleviate the other in herself. Upon him, there-she expended a certain, or rather an uncertain kind of affection, which, if it might have been more fittingly spent upon a lapdog, and was worth but little, might yet have become worth everything, had she been moderately good.

Hugh did not see Euphra again for more than a fortnight.

CHAPTER XXX.

CHANGES.

Hey, and the rue grows bonny wi' thyme!
And the thyme it is withered, and rue is in prime.

Refrain of an old Scotch song, altered by BURNS.

He hath wronged me; indeed he hath;—at a word, he hath;—believe me; Robert Shallow, Esquire, saith he is wronged.

Merry Wives of Windsor.

AT length, one evening, entering the drawing-room before dinner, Hugh found Euphra there alone. He bowed with embarrassment, and uttered some commonplace congratulation on her recovery. She answered him gently and coldly. Her whole air and appearance were signs of acute suffering. She did not make the slightest approach to their former familiarity, but she spoke without any embarrassment, like one who had given herself up, and was, therefore, indifferent. Hugh could not help feeling as if she knew every thought that was passing in his mind, and, having withdrawn herself from him, was watching him with a cold, ghostly interest. She took his arm to go into the dining-room, and actually leaned upon it, as, indeed, she was compelled to do. Her uncle was delighted to see her once more. Mrs. Elton addressed her with kindness, and Lady Emily with sweet cordiality. She herself seemed to care for nobody and nothing. As soon as dinner was over, she sent for her maid, and withdrew to her own room. It was a great relief to Hugh to feel that he was no longer in danger of encountering her eyes.

Gradually she recovered strength, though it was again some days before she appeared at the dinner-table. The distance between Hugh and her seemed to increase instead of diminish, till at length he scarcely dared to offer her the smallest civility, lest she should despise him as a hypocrite. The further she removed herself from him, the more he felt inclined to respect her. By common consent they avoided, as much as before, any behaviour that might attract attention; though the effort was of a very different nature now. It was wretched enough, no doubt, for both of them.

The time drew near for Lady Emily's departure.

"What are your plans for the winter, Mrs. Elton?" said Mr. Arnold, one day

"I intend spending the winter in London," she answered.

"Then you are not going with Lady Emily to Madeira?"

"No. Her father and one of her sisters are going with her."

"I have a great mind to spend the winter abroad myself; but the difficulty is what to do with Harry."

"Could you not leave him with Mr. Sutherland?"

"No. I do not choose to do that."

"Then let him come to me. I shall have all my little establishment up, and there will be plenty of room for Harry."

"A very kind offer. I may possibly avail myself of it."

"I fear we could hardly accommodate his tutor, though. But that will be very easily arranged. He could sleep out of the house, could he not?"

"Give yourself no trouble about that. I wish Harry to have masters for the various branches he will study. It will teach him more of men and the world generally, and prevent his being too much influenced by one style of thinking."

"But Mr. Sutherland is a very good tutor."

"Yes. Very."

To this there could be no reply but a question; and Mr. Arnold's manner not inviting one, the conversation was dropped.

Euphra gradually resumed her duties in the

house, as far as great lameness would permit. She continued to show a quiet and dignified reserve towards Hugh. She made no attempts to fascinate him, and never avoided his look when it chanced to meet hers. But although there was no reproach any more than fascination in her eyes, Hugh's always fell before hers. She walked softly like Ahab, as if, now that Hugh knew, she, too, was ever conscious.

Her behaviour to Mrs. Elton and Lady Emily was likewise improved, but apparently only from an increase of indifference. When the time came, and they departed, she did not even appear to be much relieved.

Once she asked Hugh to help her with a passage of Dante, but betrayed no memory of the past. His pleased haste to assist her, showed that he at least, if fancy-free, was not memory-clear. She thanked him very gently and truly, took up her book like a school-girl, and limped away. Hugh was smitten to the heart. "If I could but do something for her!" thought he; but there was nothing to be done.

Although she had deserved it, somehow her behaviour made him feel as if he had wronged her in ceasing to love her.

One day, in the end of September, Mr. Arnold and Hugh were alone after breakfast. Mr. Arnold spoke:

"Mr. Sutherland, I have altered my plans with regard to Harry. I wish him to spend the winter in London."

Hugh listened and waited. Mr. Arnold went on, after a slight pause:

"There I wish him to reap such advantages as are to be gained in the metropolis. He has improved wonderfully under your instruction; and is now, I think, to be benefited principally by a variety of teachers. I therefore intend that he shall have masters for the different branches which it is desirable he should study. Consequently I shall be compelled to deny him your services, valuable as they have hitherto been."

"Very well, Mr. Arnold," said Mr. Sutherland, with the indifference of one who feels himself ill-used. "When shall I take my leave of him?"

"Not before the middle of the next month, at the earliest. But I will write you a cheque for your salary at once."

So saying, Mr. Arnold left the room for a moment, and returning, handed Hugh a cheque for a year's salary. Hugh glanced at it, and offering it again to Mr. Arnold, said:

"No, Mr. Arnold; I can claim scarcely more than half a year's salary."

"Mr. Sutherland, your engagement was at so much a year; and if I prevent you from fulfilling your part of it, I am bound to fulfil mine. Indeed, you might claim further provision."

"You are very kind, Mr. Arnold."

"Only just," rejoined Mr. Arnold, with conscious dignity. "I am under great obligation to you for the way in which you have devoted yourself to Harry."

Hugh's conscience gave him a pang. Is anything more painful than undeserved praise?

"I have hardly done my duty by him," said he.

"I can only say that the boy is wonderfully altered for the better, and I thank you. I am obliged to you: oblige me by putting the cheque in your pocket."

Hugh persisted no longer in his refusal; and indeed it had been far more a feeling of pride than of justice that made him decline accepting it at first. Nor was there any generosity in Mr. Arnold's cheque; for Hugh, as he admitted, might have claimed board and lodging as well. But Mr. Arnold was one of the ordinarily honourable, who, with perfect characters for uprightness, always contrive to err on the safe side of the purse, and the doubtful side of a severely interpreted obligation. Such people, in so doing, not unfrequently secure for themselves, at the same time, the reputation of generosity.

Hugh could not doubt that his dismissal was somehow or other connected with the loss of the ring; but he would not stoop to inquire into the matter. He hoped that time would set all right; and, in fact, felt considerable indifference to the opinion of Mr. Arnold, or of any one in the house, except Harry.

The boy burst into tears when informed of his father's decision with regard to his winter studies, and could only be consoled by the hope which Hugh held out to him—certainly upon a very slight foundation—that they might meet sometimes in London. For the little time that remained, Hugh devoted himself unceasingly to his pupil; not merely studying with him, but walking, riding, reading stories, and going through all sorts of exercises for the strengthening of his person and constitution. The best results followed both for Harry and his tutor.

CHAPTER XXXI.

EXPLANATIONS.

I have done nothing good to win belief,
My life hath been so faithless; all the creatures
Made for heaven's honours, have their ends, and good ones;
All but . . . . false women . . . . When they die, like tales
Ill-told, and unbelieved, they pass away.

. . . .

I will redeem one minute of my age,
Or, like another Niobe, I'll weep
Till I am water.

BEAUMONT AND FLETCHER.—*The Maid's Tragedy.*

THE days passed quickly by; and the last evening that Hugh was to spend at Arnstead arrived. He wandered out alone. He had been with Harry all day, and now he wished for a few moments of solitude. It was a lovely autumn evening. He went into the woods behind the house. The leaves were still thick upon the trees, but most of them had changed to gold, and brown, and red; and the sweet faint odours of those that had fallen, and lay thick underfoot, ascended like a voice from the grave, saying: "Here dwelleth some sadness, but no despair." As he strolled about among them, the whole history of his past life arose before him. This often happens before any change in our history, and is surest to take place at the approach of the greatest change of all, when we are about to pass into the unknown, whence we came.

In this mood, it was natural that his sins should rise before him. They came as the shadows of his best pleasures. For now, in looking back, he could fix on no period of his history, around which the aureole, which glorifies the sacred things of the past, had gathered in so golden a hue, as around the memory of the holy cottage, the temple in which abode David, and Janet, and Margaret. All the story glided past, as the necromantic Will called up the sleeping dead in the mausoleum of the brain. And that solemn, kingly, gracious old man, who had been to him a father, he had forgotten; the homely tenderness which, from fear of its own force, concealed itself behind a humorous roughness of manner, he had—no, not despised—but forgotten, too; and if the dim pearly loveliness of the trustful, grateful maiden had not been quite forgotten, yet she too had been neglected, had died, as it were, and been buried in the churchyard of the past, where the grass grows long over the graves, and the moss soon begins to fill up the chiselled records. He was ungrateful. He dared not allow to himself that he was unloving; but he must confess himself ungrateful.

Musing sorrowfully and self-reproachfully, he came to the Ghost's Avenue. Up and down its aisle he walked, a fit place for remembering the past, and the sins of the present. Yielding himself to what thoughts might arise, the strange sight he had seen here on that moonlit night, of two silent wandering figures—or could it be that they were one and the same, suddenly changed in hue?—returned upon him. This vision had been so speedily followed by the second and more alarming apparition of Lady Euphrasia, that he had hardly had time to speculate on what the former could have been. He was meditating upon all these strange events, and remarking to himself that, since his midnight encounter with Lady Euphrasia, the house had been as quiet as a church-yard at noon, when all suddenly, he saw before him, at some little distance, a dark figure approaching him. His heart seemed to bound into his throat and choke him, as he said to himself: "It is the nun again!" But the next moment he saw that it was Euphra. I do not know which he would have preferred not meeting alone, and in the deepening twilight: Euphra, too, had become like a ghost to him. His first impulse was to turn aside into the wood, but she had seen him, and was evidently going to address him. He therefore advanced to meet her. She spoke first, approaching him with painful steps.

"I have been looking for you, Mr. Sutherland. I wanted very much to have a little conversation with you before you go. Will you allow me?"

Hugh felt like a culprit directly. Euphra's manner was quite collected and kind; yet through it all a consciousness showed itself, that the relation which had once existed between them had passed away for ever. In her voice there was something like the tone of wind blowing through a ruin.

"I shall be most happy," said he.

She smiled sadly. A great change had passed upon her.

"I am going to be quite open with you," she said. "I am perfectly aware, as well as you are, that the boyish fancy you had for me is gone. Do not be offended. You are manly enough, but your love for me was boyish. Most first loves are childish, quite irrespective of age. I do not blame you in the least."

This seemed to Hugh rather a strange style to assume, if all was true that his own eyes had reported. She went on:

"Nor must you think it has cost me much to lose it."

Hugh felt hurt, at which no one who understands will be surprised.

"But I cannot afford to lose *you*, the only friend I have," she added.

Hugh turned towards her with a face full of manhood and truth.

"You shall not lose me, Euphra, if you will be honest to yourself and to me."

"Thank you. I can trust you. I will be honest."

At that moment, without the revival of a trace of his former feelings, Hugh felt nearer to her than he had ever felt before. Now there seemed to be truth between them, the only medium through which beings can unite.

"I fear I have wronged you much," she

went on. "I do not mean some time ago." Here she hesitated.—"I fear I am the cause of your leaving Arnstead."

"You, Euphra? No. You must be mistaken."

"I think not. But I am compelled to make an unwilling disclosure of a secret—a sad secret about myself. Do not hate me quite—I am a somnambulist."

She hid her face in her hands, as if the night which had now closed around them did not hide her enough. Hugh did not reply. Absorbed in the interest which both herself and her confession aroused in him, he could only listen eagerly. She went on, after a moment's pause:

"I did not think at first that I had taken the ring. I thought another had. But last night, and not till then, I discovered that I was the culprit."

"How?"

"That requires explanation. I have no recollection of the events of the previous night when I have been walking in my sleep. Indeed, the utter absence of a sense of dreaming always makes me suspect that I have been wandering. But sometimes I have a vivid dream, which I know, though I can give no proof of it, to be a reproduction of some previous somnambulic experience. Do not ask me to recall the horrors I dreamed last night. I am sure I took the ring."

"Then you dreamed what you did with it?"

"Yes, I gave it to——"

Here her voice sank and ceased. Hugh would not urge her.

"Have you mentioned this to Mr. Arnold?"

"No. I do not think it would do any good. But I will, if you wish it," she added submissively.

"Not at all. Just as you think best."

"I could not tell him everything. I cannot tell you everything. If I did, Mr. Arnold would turn me out of the house. I am a very unhappy girl, Mr. Sutherland."

From the tone of these words, Hugh could

not for a moment suppose that Euphra had any remaining design of fascination in them.

"Perhaps he might want to keep you, if I told him all; but I do not think, after the way he has behaved to you, that you could stay with him, for he would never apologize. It is very selfish of me; but indeed I have not the courage to confess to him."

"I assure you nothing could make me remain now. But what can I do for you?"

"Only let me depend upon you, in case I should need your help; or ——"

Here Euphra stopped suddenly, and caught hold of Hugh's left hand, which he had lifted to brush an insect from his face.

"Where is your ring?" she said, in a tone of suppressed anxiety.

"Gone, Euphra. My father's ring! It was lying beside Lady Euphrasia's."

Euphra's face was again hidden in her hands. She sobbed and moaned like one in despair. When she grew a little calmer, she said:

"I am sure I did not take *your* ring, dear Hugh—I am not a thief. I had a kind of right to the other, and he said it ought to have been his, for his real name was Count von Halkar—the same name as Lady Euphrasia's before she was married. *He* took it, I am sure."

"It was he that knocked me down in the dark that night then, Euphra."

"Did he? Oh! I shall have to tell you all. —That wretch has a terrible power over me. I loved him once. But I refused to take the ring from your desk, because I knew it would get you into trouble. He threw me into a somnambulic sleep, and sent me for the ring. But I should have remembered if I had taken yours. Even in my sleep, I don't think he could have made me do that. You may know I speak the truth, when I am telling my own disgrace. He promised to set me free if I would get the ring; but he has not done it, and he will not."

Sobs again interrupted her.

"I was afraid your ring was gone. I don't know why I thought so, except that you hadn't it on, when you came to see me. Or perhaps it was because I am sometimes forced to think what that wretch is thinking. He made me go to him that night you saw me, Hugh. But I was so ill, I don't think I should have been able, but that I could not rest till I had asked him about your ring. He said he knew nothing about it."

"I am sure he has it," said Hugh. And he related to Euphra the struggle he had had with Funkelstein and its result. She shuddered.

"I have been a devil to you, Hugh; I have betrayed you to *him*. You will never see your ring again. Here, take mine. It is not so good as yours, but for the sake of the old way you thought of me, take it."

"No, no, Euphra; Mr. Arnold would miss it. Besides, you know it would not be my father's ring, and it was not for the value of the diamond I cared most about it. And I am not sure that I shall not find it again. I am going up to London, where I shall fall in with him, I hope."

"But do take care of yourself. He has no conscience. God knows, I have had little, but he has none."

"I know he has none; but a conscience is not a bad auxiliary, and there I shall have some advantage of him. But what could he want that ring of Lady Euphrasia's for?"

"I don't know. He never told me."

"It was not worth much."

"Next to nothing."

"I shall be surer to find that than my own. And I will find it, if I can, that Mr. Arnold may believe I was not to blame."

"Do. But be careful."

"Don't fear. I will be careful."

She held out her hand, as if to take leave of him, but withdrew it again with the sudden cry:

"What *shall* I do? I thought he had left me to myself, till that night in the library."

She held down her head in silence. Then she said, slowly, in a tone of agony:

"I am a slave, body and soul.—Hugh!" she added, passionately, and looking up in his face, "do you think there is a God?"

Her eyes glimmered with the faint reflex from gathered tears, that silently overflowed.

And now Hugh's own poverty struck him with grief and humiliation. Here was a soul seeking God, and he had no right to say that there was a God, for he knew nothing about him. He had been told so; but what could that far-off witness do for the need of a desolate heart? She had been told so a million of times. He could not say that he *knew* it. That was what she wanted and needed.

He was honest, and so replied:

"I do not know. I hope so."

He felt that she was already beyond him; for she had begun to cry into the vague, seemingly heartless void, and say:

"Is there a God somewhere to hear me when I cry?"

And with all the teaching he had had, he

had no word of comfort to give. Yes, he had: he had known David Elginbrod.

Before he had shaped his thought, she said:

"I think, if there were a God, he would help me; for I am nothing but a poor slave now. I have hardly a will of my own."

The sigh she heaved told of a hopeless oppression.

"The best man, and the wisest, and the noblest I ever knew," said Hugh, "believed in God with his whole heart and soul and strength and mind. In fact, he cared for nothing but God; or rather, he cared for everything because it belonged to God. He was never afraid of anything, never vexed at anything, never troubled about anything. He *was* a good man."

Hugh was surprised at the light which broke upon the character of David, as he held it before his mind's eye, in order to describe it to Euphra. He seemed never to have understood him before.

"Ah! I wish I knew him. I would go to

that man, and ask him to save me. Where does he live?"

"Alas! I do not know whether he is alive or dead—the more to my shame. But he lives, if he lives, far away in the north of Scotland."

She paused.

"No. I could not go there. I will write to him."

Hugh could not discourage her, though he doubted whether a real communication could be established between them.

"I will write down his address for you, when I go in," said he. "But what can he save you from?"

"From no God," she answered, solemnly. "If there is no God, then I am sure that there is a devil, and that he has got me in his power."

Hugh felt her shudder, for she was leaning on his arm, she was still so lame. She continued:

"Oh! if I had a God, he would right me, I know."

Hugh could not reply. A pause followed.

"Good-bye. I feel pretty sure we shall meet again. My presentiments are generally true," said Euphra, at length.

Hugh kissed her hand with far more real devotion than he had ever kissed it with before.

She left him, and hastened to the house 'with feeble speed.' He was sorry she was gone. He walked up and down for some time, meditating on the strange girl and her strange words; till, hearing the dinner bell, he too must hasten in to dress.

Euphra met him at the dinner-table without any change of her late manner. Mr. Arnold wished him good night more kindly than usual. When he went up to his room, he found that Harry had already cried himself to sleep.

CHAPTER XXXII.

DEPARTURE.

I fancy deemed fit guide to lead my way,
And as I deemed I did pursue her track;
Wit lost his aim, and will was fancy's prey;
The rebel won, the ruler went to wrack.
But now sith fancy did with folly end,
Wit, bought with loss—will, taught by wit, will men
SOUTHWELL.—*David's Pec*

AFTER dinner, Hugh wandered over the w known places, to bid them good-bye. T he went up to his room, and, with the var of a young author, took his poems out of fatal old desk; wrote: "Take them, plea such as they are. Let me be your frien inclosed them with the writing, and addres them to Euphra. By the time he saw them again, they were so much waste-paper in his eyes.

But what were his plans for the future?

First of all, he would go to London. There he would do many things. He would try to find Funkelstein. He would write. He would make acquaintance with London life; for had he not plenty of money in his pocket? And who could live more thriftily than he?—During his last session at Aberdeen, he had given some private lessons, and so contrived to eke out his small means. These were wretchedly paid for, namely, not quite at the rate of sevenpence-halfpenny a lesson; but still that was something, where more could not be had.—Now he would try to do the same in London, where he would be much better paid. Or perhaps he might get a situation in a school for a short time, if he were driven to ultimate necessity. At all events, he would see London, and look about him for a little while, before he settled to anything definite.

With this hopeful prospect before him, he

next morning bade adieu to Arnstead. I will not describe the parting with poor Harry. The boy seemed ready to break his heart, and Hugh himself had enough ado to refrain from tears. One of the grooms drove him to the railway in the dog-cart. As they came near the station, Hugh gave him half-a-crown. Enlivened by the gift, the man began to talk.

"He's a rum customer, that ere gemman with the foring name. The colour of his puss I couldn't swear to now. *Never* saw sixpence o' his'n. My opinion is, master had better look arter *his* spoons. And for missus—well, it's a pity! He's a rum un, as I say, anyhow."

The man here nodded several times, half compassionately, half importantly.

Hugh did not choose to inquire what he meant. They reached the station, and in a few minutes he was shooting along towards London, that social vortex, which draws everything towards its central tumult.

But there is a central repose beyond the motions of the worlds; and through the turmoil of London, Hugh was journeying towards that wide stillness—that silence of the soul, which is not desolate, but rich with unutterable harmonies.

END OF BOOK II.

BOOK III.

LONDON.

Art thou poor, yet hast thou golden slumbers?
  Oh, sweet content!
Art thou rich, yet is thy mind perplexed?
  Oh, punishment!
Dost thou laugh to see how fools are vexed
To add to golden numbers, golden numbers?
  Oh, sweet content!

Work apace, apace, apace, apace;
Honest labour bears a lovely face.

Probably THOMAS DEKKER.—*Comedy of Patient Grissell.*

CHAPTER I.

LODGINGS.

Heigh ho! sing heigh ho! unto the green holly:
Most friendship is feigning, *most* loving mere folly:
Then, heigh ho! the holly!
This life is most jolly.

Song in As You Like It.

HUGH felt rather dreary as, through Bermondsey, he drew nigh to the London Bridge Station. Fog, and drizzle, and smoke, and stench composed the atmosphere. He got out in a drift of human atoms. Leaving his luggage at the office, he set out on foot to explore—in fact, to go and look for his future, which, even when he met it, he would not be able to recognize with any certainty. The first form in which he was interested to find it embodied, was that of lodgings; but where even to look, he did not know. He had been in London for a few days in the spring on his way to Arnstead, so he was not utterly ignorant of the anatomy of the monster city; but his little knowledge could not be of much service to him now. And how different it was from the London of spring, which had lingered in his memory and imagination; when, transformed by the 'heavenly alchemy' of the piercing sunbeams that slanted across the streets from chimney-tops to opposite basements, the dust and smoke showed great inclined planes of light, up whose steep slopes one longed to climb to the fountain glory whence they flowed! Now the streets, from garret to cellar, seemed like huge kennels of muddy, moist, filthy air, down through which settled the heavier particles of smoke and rain upon the miserable human beings who crawled below in the deposit, like shrimps in the tide, or whitebait at the bottom of the muddy Thames. He had to wade through deep thin mud even on the pavements. Everybody looked depressed, and hurried by with a cowed look; as if conscious that the rain and general misery were a plague drawn down on the city by his own individual crime. Nobody seemed to care for anybody or anything. "Good heavens!" thought Hugh; "what a place this must be for one without money!" It looked like a chaos of human monads. And yet, in reality, the whole mass was so bound together, interwoven, and matted, by the crossing and intertwisting threads of interest, mutual help, and relationship of every kind, that Hugh soon found how hard it was to get within the mass at all, so as to be in any degree partaker of the benefits it shared within itself.

He did not wish to get lodgings in the outskirts, for he thought that would remove him from every centre of action or employment. But he saw no lodgings anywhere. Growing tired and hungry, he went at length into an eating-house, which he thought looked cheap; and proceeded to dine upon a cinder, which had been a steak. He tried to delude himself into the idea that it was a steak still, by withdrawing his attention from it, and fixing it upon a newspaper two days old. Finding nothing of interest, he dallied with the advertisements. He soon came upon a column from which single gentlemen appeared to be in request as lodgers. Looking over these advertisements, which had more interest for him at the moment than all home and foreign news, battles and murders included, he drew a map from his pocket, and began to try to find out some of the localities indicated. Most of them were in or towards the suburbs. At last he spied one in a certain square, which, after long and diligent search, and with the assistance of the girl who waited on him, he found on his map. It was in the neighbourhood of Holborn, and, from the place it occupied in the map, seemed central enough for his vague purposes. Above all, the terms were said to be moderate. But no description of the character of the lodgings was given, else Hugh would not have ventured to look at them. What he wanted was something of the same sort as he had had in Aberdeen—a single room, or a room and bed-room, for which he should have to pay only a few shillings a week.

Refreshed by his dinner, wretched as it was, he set out again. To his great joy, the rain was over, and an afternoon sun was trying, with some slight measure of success, to pierce the clouds of the London atmosphere: it had already succeeded with the clouds of the terrene. He soon found his way into Holborn, and thence into the square in question. It looked to him very attractive; for it was quietness itself, and had no thoroughfare, except across one of its corners. True, it was invaded by the universal roar—for what place in London is not?—but it contributed little or nothing of its own manufacture to the general production of sound in the metropolis. The centre was occupied by grass and trees, inclosed within an iron railing. All the leaves were withered, and many had dropped already on the pavement below. In the middle stood the statue of a queen, of days gone by. The tide of fashion had rolled away far to the west, and yielded a free passage to the inroads of commerce, and of the general struggle for ignoble existence, upon this once favoured island in its fluctuating waters. Old windows, flush with the external walls, whence had glanced fair eyes to which fashion was even dearer than beauty, now displayed *Lodgings to Let* between knitted curtains, from which all idea of drapery had been expelled by severe starching. Amongst these he soon found the house he sought, and shrunk from its important size and bright equipments; but, summoning courage, thought it better to ring the bell. A withered old lady, in just the same stage of decay as the square, and adorned after the same fashion as the house, came to the door, cast a doubtful look at Hugh, and when he had stated his object, asked him, in a hard, keen, unmodulated voice, to walk in. He followed her, and found himself in a dining-room, which to him, judging by his purse, and not by what he had been used to of late, seemed sumptuous. He said at once:

"It is needless for me to trouble you further. I see your rooms will not suit me."

The old lady looked annoyed.

"Will you see the drawing-room apartments, then?" she said, crustily.

"No, thank you. It would be giving you quite unnecessary trouble."

"My apartments have always given satisfaction, I assure you, sir."

"Indeed, I have no reason to doubt it. I wish I could afford to take them," said Hugh, thinking it better to be open than to hurt her feelings. "I am sure I should be very comfortable. But a poor——"

He did not know what to call himself.

"O-oh!" said the landlady. Then, after a pause—"Well?" interrogatively.

"Well, I was a tutor last, but I don't know what I may be next."

She kept looking at him. Once or twice she looked at him from head to foot.

"You are respectable?"

"I hope so," said Hugh, laughing.

"Well!"—this time not interrogatively.

"How many rooms would you like?"

"The fewer the better. Half a one, if there were nobody in the other half."

"Well!—And you wouldn't give much trouble, I daresay."

"Only for coals and water to wash and drink."

"And you wouldn't dine at home?"

"No—nor anywhere else," said Hugh; but the second and larger clause was *sotto voce.*

"And you wouldn't smoke in-doors?"

"No."

"And you would wipe your boots clean before you went up-stairs?"

"Yes, certainly." Hugh was beginning to be exceedingly amused, but he kept his gravity wonderfully.

"Have you any money?"

"Yes; plenty for the meantime. But when I shall get more, I don't know, you see."

"Well, I've a room at the top of the house, which I'll make comfortable for you; and you may stay as long as you like to behave yourself."

"But what is the rent?"

"Four shillings a week—to you. Would you like to see it?"

"Yes, if you please."

She conducted him up to the third floor, and showed him a good-sized room, rather bare, but clean.

"This will do delightfully," said Hugh.

"I will make it a little more comfortable for you, you know."

"Thank you very much. Shall I pay you a month in advance?"

"No, no," she answered, with a grim smile. "I might want to get rid of you, you know. It must be a week's warning, no more."

"Very well. I have no objection. I will go and fetch my luggage. I suppose I may come in at once?"

"The sooner the better, young man, in a

place like London. The sooner you come home the better pleased I shall be. There now!"

So saying, she walked solemnly down-stairs before him, and let him out. Hugh hurried away to fetch his luggage, delighted that he had so soon succeeded in finding just what he wanted. As he went, he speculated on the nature of his landlady, trying to account for her odd rough manner, and the real kindness of her rude words. He came to the conclusion that she was naturally kind to profusion, and that this kindness had, some time or other, perhaps repeatedly, been taken shameful advantage of; that at last she had come to the resolution to defend herself by means of a general misanthropy, and supposed that she had succeeded, when she had got no further than to have so often imitated the tone of her own behaviour when at its crossest, as to have made it habitual by repetition.

In all probability some unknown sympathy had drawn her to Hugh. She might have had a son about his age, who had run away thirty years ago. Or rather, for she seemed an old maid, she had been jilted some time by a youth about the same size as Hugh; and therefore she loved him the moment she saw him. Or, in short, a thousand things. Certainly seldom have lodgings been let so oddly or so cheaply. But some impulse or other of the whimsical old human heart, which will have its way, was satisfied therein.

When he returned in a couple of hours, with his boxes on the top of a cab, the door was opened, before he knocked, by a tidy maid, who, without being the least like her mistress, yet resembled her excessively. She helped him to carry his boxes up-stairs; and when he reached his room, he found a fire burning cheerily, a muffin down before it, a tea-kettle singing on the hob, and the tea-tray set upon a nice white cloth on a table right in front of the fire, with an old-fashioned high-backed easy-chair by its side—the very chair to go to sleep in over a novel. The old lady soon made her appearance, with the teapot in one hand, and a plate of butter in the other.

"Oh! thank you," said Hugh. "This *is* comfortable!"

She answered only by compressing her lips till her mouth vanished altogether, and nodding her head as much as to say: "I know it is. I intended it should be." She then poured water into the teapot, set it down by the fire, and vanished.

Hugh sat down in the easy-chair, and resolved to be comfortable, at least till he had had his tea; after which he would think what he was to do next. A knock at the door—and his landlady entered, laid a penny newspaper on the table, and went away. This was just what he wanted to complete his comfort. He took it up, and read while he consumed his bread and butter. When he had had enough of tea and newspaper, he said to himself:

"Now, what am I to do next?"

It is a happy thing for us that this is really

all we have to concern ourselves about—what to do *next.* No man *can* do the second thing. He can do the first. If he omits it, the wheels of the social Juggernaut roll over him, and leave him more or less crushed behind. If he does it, he keeps in front, and finds room to do the next again; and so he is sure to arrive at something, for the onward march will carry him with it. There is no saying to what perfection of success a man may come, who begins with what he can do, and uses the means at his hand. He makes a vortex of action, however slight, towards which all the means instantly begin to gravitate. Let a man but lay hold of something—anything, and he is in the high road to success—though it may be very long before he can walk comfortably in it.—It is true the success may be measured out according to a standard very different from his.

But in Hugh's case, the difficulty was to grasp anything—to make a beginning anywhere. He knew nobody; and the globe of society seemed like a mass of adamant, on which he could not gain the slightest hold, or make the slightest impression. Who would introduce him to pupils? Nobody. He had the testimonials of his professors; but who would ask to see them?—His eye fell on the paper. He would advertise.

CHAPTER II.

LETTERS FOR THE POST.

Nothing but drought and dearth, but bush and brake,
  Which way soe'er I look, I see.
Some may dream merrily, but when they wake,
  They dress themselves, and come to thee.

GEORGE HERBERT.—*Home.*

HE got his writing materials, and wrote to the effect, that a graduate of a Scotch university was prepared to give private lessons in the classics and mathematics, or even in any of the inferior branches of education, &c., &c. This he would take to the *Times* next day.

As soon as he had done this, Duty lifted up her head, and called him. He obeyed, and wrote to his mother. Duty called again; and he wrote, though with much trepidation and humiliation, to David Elginbrod.

It was a good beginning. He had commenced his London life in doing what he knew he ought to do. His trepidation in writing to David, arose in part, it must be confessed, from the strange result of one of the experiments at Arnstead.

This was his letter. But he sat and meditated a long time before he began it.

"MY DEAR FRIEND,—If I did not think you would forgive me, I should feel, now that I have once allowed my mind to rest upon my conduct to you, as if I could never hold up my head again. After much occupation of thought and feeling with other things, a season of silence has come, and my sins look me in the face. First of them all is my neglect of you, to whom I owe more than to any man else, except, perhaps, my father. Forgive me, for forgiveness' sake. You know it takes a long time for a child to know its mother. It takes everything as a matter of course, till suddenly one day it lifts up its eyes, and knows that a face is looking at it. I have been like the child towards you; but I am beginning to feel what you have been to me. I want to be good. I am very lonely now in great noisy London. Write to me, if you please, and comfort me. I wish I were as good as you. Then everything would go right with me. Do not suppose that I am in great trouble of any kind. As yet I am very comfortable, as far as external circumstances go. But I have a kind of aching inside me. Something is not right, and I want your help. You will know what I mean. What am I to do? Please to remember me in the kindest, most grateful manner to Mrs. Elginbrod and Margaret. It is more than I deserve, but I hope they have not forgotten me as I have seemed to forget them.

"I am, my dear Mr. Elginbrod,

"Your old friend,

"HUGH SUTHERLAND."

I may as well insert here another letter, which arrived at Turriepuffit, likewise addressed to David, some six weeks after the foregoing. They were both taken to Janet, of course:

"SIR,—I have heard from one who knows you, that you believe—really believe in God. That is why I write to you. It may seem very strange in me to do so, but how can I help it? I am a very unhappy woman, for I am in the power of a bad man. I cannot explain it all to you, and I will not attempt it; for sometimes I almost think I am out of my mind, and that it is all a delusion. But, alas! delusion or not, it is a dreadful reality to me in all its consequences. It is of such a nature that no one can help me—but God, if there be a God; and if you can make me believe that there is a God, I shall not need to be persuaded that he will help me; for I will besiege him with prayers night and day to set me free. And even if I am out of my mind, who can help me but him? Ah! is it not when we are driven to despair, when there is no more help anywhere, that we look around for some power of good that can put right all that is wrong? Tell me, dear sir, what to do. Tell me that there certainly is a God; else I shall die raving. He said you knew about him better than anybody else.

"I am, honoured Sir,

"Your obedient servant,

"EUPHRASIA CAMERON.

"Arnstead, Surrey, &c., &c."

David's answer to this letter, would have been something worth having. But I think it would have been all summed up in one word: Try and see: call and listen.

But what could Janet do with such letters? She did the only thing she could: she sent them to Margaret.

Hugh found it no great hardship to go to bed in the same room in which he sat. The bed looked peculiarly inviting; for, strange to tell, it was actually hung with the same pattern of old-fashioned chintz, as the bed which had been his from his earliest recollection, till he left his father's house. How could he mistake the trees, growing with tufts to the ground, or the great birds which he used to think were crows, notwithstanding their red and yellow plumage? It was all over red, brown, and yellow. He could remember, and reconstruct the very faces, distorted and awful, which, in the delirium of childish sicknesses, he used to discover in the foliage and stems of the trees. It made the whole place seem to him homely and kind. When he got tired, he knelt by his bedside, which he had not done for a long time, and then went to bed. Hardship! No. It was very pleasant to see the dying fire, and his books about and his papers; and to dream, half-asleep and half-awake, that the house-fairies were stealing out to gambol for a little in the fire-lighted silence of the room as he slept, and to vanish as the embers turned black. He had not been so happy for a long time as now. The writing of that letter had removed a load from his heart. True, we can never be at peace till we have performed the highest duty of all—till we have arisen, and gone to our Father; but the performance of smaller duties, yes, even of the smallest, will do more to give us temporary repose, will act more as healthful anodynes, than the greatest joys that can come to us from any other quarter. He soon fell asleep, and dreamed that he was a little child, lost in a snow-storm; and that just as the snow had reached above his head, and he was beginning to be smothered, a great hand caught hold of him by the arm and lifted him out; and, lo! the storm had ceased, and the stars were sparkling overhead like diamonds that had been drinking the light of the sun all day; and he saw that it was David, as strong as ever, who had rescued him, the little child, and was leading him home to Janet. But he got sleepy and faint upon the way, which was long and cold; and then David lifted him up and carried him in his bosom, and he fell asleep. When he woke, and, opening his eyes, looked up to him who bore him, it was David no longer. The face was that which was marred more than any man's, because the soul within had loved more; it was the face of the Son of Man, and he was carrying him like a lamb in his bosom. He gazed more and more as they travelled through the cold night; and the joy of lying in the embrace of that man, grew and grew, till it became too strong for the bonds of sleep; and he awoke in the fog of a London morning.

CHAPTER III.

ENDEAVOURS.

And, even should misfortunes come,
—I, here wha sit, hae met wi' some,
An's thankfu' for them yet.
They gie the wit of age to youth;
They let us ken oursel';
They mak' us see the naked truth,
The real guid and ill.
Tho' losses, and crosses,
Be lessons right severe,
There's wit there, ye'll get there,
Ye'll find nae other where.

BURNS.

HUGH took his advertisement to the *Times* office, and paid what seemed to him an awful amount for its insertion. Then he wandered about London till the middle of the day, when he went into a baker's shop, and bought two penny loaves, which he put in his pocket. Having found his way to the British Museum, he devoured them at his leisure as he walked through the Grecian and Roman saloons. "What is the use of good health," he said to himself, "if a man cannot live upon bread?" Porridge and oatmeal cakes would have pleased him as well; but that food for horses is not so easily procured in London, and costs more than the other. A cousin of his had lived in Edinburgh for six months upon eighteen-pence a week in that way, and had slept the greater part of the time upon the floor, training himself for the hardships of a soldier's life. And he could not forget the college youth whom his comrades had considered mean, till they learned that, out of his poor bursary of fourteen pounds a session, and what he could make besides by private teaching at the rate previously mentioned or even less, he helped his parents to educate a younger brother; and, in order to do so, lived himself upon oatmeal and potatoes. But they did not find this out till after he was dead, poor fellow! He could not stand it.

I ought at the same time to mention, that Hugh rarely made use of a crossing on a muddy day, without finding a half-penny somewhere about him for the sweeper. He would rather walk through oceans of mud, than cross at the natural place when he had no coppers—especially if he had patent leather boots on.

After he had eaten his bread, he went home to get some water. Then, as he had nothing else to do, he sat down in his room, and began to manufacture a story, thinking it just possible it might be accepted by one or other of the pseudo-literary publications with which London is inundated in hebdomadal floods. He found spinning almost as easy as if he had been a spider, for he had a ready invention, and a natural gift of speech; so that, in a few days, he had finished a story, quite as good as most of those that appear in the better sort of weekly publications. This, in his modesty, he sent to one of the inferior sort, and heard nothing more of it than if he had flung it into the sea. Possibly he flew too low. He tried again, but with no better success. His ambition grew with his disappointments, or perhaps rather with the exercise of his faculties. Before many days had passed, he made up his mind to try a novel. For three months he worked at this six hours a day regularly. When material failed him, from the exhaustion consequent upon uninterrupted production, he would recreate himself by lying fallow for an hour or two, or walking out in a mood for merely passive observation. But this anticipates.

His advertisement did not produce a single inquiry, and he shrunk from spending more money in such an apparently unprofitable appliance. Day after day went by, and no voice reached him from the unknown world of labour. He went at last to several stationers' shops in the neighbourhood, bought some necessary articles, and took these opportunities of asking if they knew of any one in want of such assistance as he could give. But unpleasant as he felt it to make such inquiries, he soon found that to most people it was equally unpleasant to reply to them. There seemed to be something disreputable in having to answer such questions, to judge from the constrained, indifferent, and sometimes, though not often, surly answers which he received. "Can it be," thought Hugh, "as disgraceful to ask for work as to ask for bread?" If he had had a thousand a year, and had wanted a situation of another thousand, it would have been quite commendable; but to try to elude cold and hunger by inquiring after paltry shilling's worths of hard labour, was despicable.

So he placed the more hope upon his novel, and worked at that diligently. But he did not find it quite so easy as he had at first expected. No one finds anything either so easy or so difficult as, in opposite moods, he had expected to find it. Everything is possible; but without labour and failure nothing is achievable. The labour, however, comes naturally, and experience grows without agonizing transitions; while the failure generally points, in its detected cause, to the way of future success. He worked on.

He did not, however, forget the ring. Frequent were his meditations, in the pauses of his story, and when walking in the streets, as to the best means of recovering it. I should rather say *any* means than *best;* for it was not yet a question of choice and degrees. The count could not but have known that the ring was of no money value; therefore it was not likely that he had stolen it in order to part with it again. Consequently it would be of no use to advertise it, or to search for it in the pawnbrokers' or second-hand jewellers' shops. To find the crystal, it was clear as itself that he must first find the count.

But how?—He could think of no plan. Any alarm would place the count on the defensive, and the jewel at once beyond reach. Besides, he wished to keep the whole matter quiet, and gain his object without his or any other name coming before the public. Therefore he would not venture to apply to the police, though doubtless they would be able to discover the man, if he were anywhere in London. He surmised that in all probability they knew him already. But he could not come to any conclusion as to the object he must have had in view in securing such a trifle.

Hugh had all but forgotten the count's cheque for a hundred guineas; for, in the first place, he had never intended presenting it—the repugnance which some minds feel to using money which they have neither received by gift nor acquired by honest earning, being at least equal to the pleasure other minds feel in gaining it without the expense of either labour or obligation; and in the second place, since he knew more about the drawer, he had felt sure that it would be of no use to present it. To make this latter conviction a certainty, he did present it, and found that there were no effects.

CHAPTER IV.

A LETTER FROM THE POST.

Hipolito. Is your wife then departed?
Orlando. She's an old dweller in those high countries, yet not from me: here, she's here; a good couple are seldom parted.—DEKKER.

WHAT wonderful things letters are! In trembling and hope the fingers unclasp, and the folded sheet drops into—no, not the post-office letter-box—but into space.

I have read a story somewhere of a poor child that dropped a letter into the post-office, addressed to *Jesus Christ in Heaven.* And it reached him, and the child had her answer. For was it not Christ present in the good man or woman—I forget the particulars of the story—who sent the child the help she needed? There was no necessity for him to answer in person, as in the case of Abgarus, king of Edessa.

Out of space from somewhere comes the answer. Such letters as those given in a previous chapter, are each a spirit-cry sent out, like a Noah's dove, into the abyss; and the spirit turns its ear, where its mouth had been turned before, and leans listening for the spirit-echo—the echo with a soul in it—the answering voice which out of the abyss will enter by the gate now turned to receive it. Whose will be the voice? What will be the sense? What chords on the harp of life have been struck afar off by the arrow-words of the letter? What tones will they send back to the longing, hungering ear? The mouth hath spoken, that the fainting ear may be filled by the return of its words through the alembic of another soul.

One cause of great uneasiness to Hugh was,

that, for some time after a reply might have been expected, he received no answer from David Elginbrod. At length, however, a letter arrived, upon the hand-writing of which he speculated in vain, perplexed with a resemblance in it to some writing that he knew; and when he opened it, he found the following answer to his own:

"DEAR MR. SUTHERLAND,—Your letter to my father has been sent to me by my mother, for what you will feel to be the sad reason, that he is no more in this world. But I cannot say it is so *very* sad to me to think that he is gone home, where my mother and I will soon join him. True love can wait well. Nor indeed, dear Mr. Sutherland, must you be too much troubled that your letter never reached him. My father was like God in this, that he always forgave anything the moment there was anything to forgive; for when else could there be such a good time?—although, of course, the person forgiven could not know it till he asked for forgiveness. But, dear Mr. Sutherland, if you could see me smiling as I write, and could yet see how earnest my heart is in writing it, I would venture to say that, in virtue of my knowing my father as I do—for I am sure I know his very soul, as near as *human* love could know it—I forgive you, in his name, for anything and everything with which you reproach yourself in regard to him. Ah! how much I owe you! And how much he used to say he owed you! We shall thank you one day, when we all meet.

"I am, dear Mr. Sutherland,

"Your grateful scholar,

"MARGARET ELGINBROD."

Hugh burst into tears on reading this letter, —with no overpowering sense of his own sin, for he felt that he was forgiven; but with a sudden insight into the beauty and grandeur of the man whom he had neglected, and the wondrous loveliness which he had transmitted from the feminine part of his nature to the wholly feminine and therefore delicately powerful nature of Margaret. The vision he had beheld in the library at Arnstead, about which, as well as about many other things that had happened to him there, he could form no theory capable of embracing all the facts—this vision returned to his mind's eye, and he felt that the glorified face he had beheld must surely have been Margaret's, whether he had seen it in the body or out of the body: such a face alone seemed to him worthy of the writer of this letter. Purposely or not, there was no address given in it; and to his surprise, when he examined the envelope with the utmost care, he could discover no postmark but the London one. The date-stamp likewise showed that it must have been posted in London.

"So," said he to himself, "in my quest of a devil, I may cross the track of an angel, who knows? But how can she be here?"

To this of course he had no answer at hand.

CHAPTER V.

BEGINNINGS.

Since a man is bound no farther to himself than to do wisely, chance is only to trouble them that stand upon chance.—SIR PHILIP SIDNEY.—*The Arcadia.*

MEANTIME a feeble star, but sparkling some rays of comfort, began to shine upon Hugh's wintry prospects. This star arose in a grocer's shop. For one day his landlady, whose grim attentions had been increasing rather than diminishing, addressed him suddenly as she was removing his breakfast apparatus. This was a very extraordinary event, for she seldom addressed him at all; and replied, when he addressed her, only in the briefest manner possible.

"Have you got any pupils yet, Mr. Sutherland?"

"No—I am sorry to say. But how did you come to know I wanted any, Miss Talbot?"

"You shouldn't have secrets at home, Mr. Sutherland. I like to know what concerns my own family, and I generally find out."

"You saw my advertisement, perhaps?"

To this suggestion Miss Talbot made no other answer than the usual compression of her lips.

"You wouldn't be above teaching a tradesman's son to begin with?"

"Certainly not. I should be very happy. Do you know of such a pupil?"

"Well, I can't exactly say I do know or I don't know; but I happened to mention to my grocer round the corner that you wanted pupils. Don't suppose, Mr. Sutherland, that I'm in the way of talking about any young men of mine; but—— "

"Not for a moment," interrupted Hugh; and Miss Talbot resumed, evidently gratified.

"Well, if you wouldn't mind stepping round the corner, I shouldn't wonder if you might make an arrangement with Mr. Appleditch. He said you might call upon him if you liked."

Hugh jumped up, and got his hat at once; received the few necessary directions from Miss Talbot, and soon found the shop. There were a good many poor people in it, buying sugar, and soap, &c.; and one lady apparently giving a large order. A young man came to Hugh, and bent over the counter in a recipient position, like a live point of interrogation. Hugh answered—

"Mr. Appleditch."

"Mr. Appleditch will be disengaged in a few minutes. Will you take a seat?"

The grocer was occupied with the lady and her order; but as soon as she departed, he approached Hugh behind the rampart, and stood towards him in the usual retail attitude.

"My name is Sutherland."

"Sutherland?" said Mr. Appleditch; "I

think I've 'eard the name somewheres, but I don't know the face."

"Miss Talbot mentioned me to you, I understand, Mr. Appleditch."

"Oh! ah! I remember. I beg your pardon. Will you step this way, Mr. Sutherland?"

Hugh followed him through a sort of drawbridge which he lifted in the counter, into a little appendix at the back of the shop. Mr. Appleditch was a meek-looking man, with large eyes, plump pasty cheeks, and a thin little person.

"'Ow de do, Mr. Sutherland?" said he, holding out his hand, as soon as they had reached this retreat.

"Thank you—quite well;" answered Sutherland, shaking hands with him as well as he could, the contact not being altogether pleasant.

"So you want pupils, do you, sir?"

"Yes."

"Ah! well, you see, sir, pupils is scarce at

this season. They ain't to be bought in every shop—ha! ha!" (The laugh was very mild.) "But I think Mrs. Appleditch could find you one, if you could agree with her about the charge, you know, and all that."

"How old is he? A boy, I suppose?"

"Well, you're right, sir. It is a boy. Not very old, though. My Samuel is just ten, but a wonderful forward boy for his years—bless him!"

"And what would you wish him to learn?"

"Oh! Latin and Greek, and all that. We intend bringing him up for the ministry.—I hope your opinions are decided, sir?"

"On some points, they are. But I do not know to what you refer, exactly."

"I mean theological opinions, sir."

"But I shall not have to teach your little boy theology."

"Certainly not, sir. That department belongs to his mother and I. Unworthy vessels, sir; mere earthen vessels; but filled with the grace of God, I hope, sir."

The grocer parted his hands, which he had been rubbing together during this conversation, and lifted them upwards from the wrists, like the fins of a seal; then dropping them, fell to rubbing them again.

"I hope so. Well—you know the best way will be for me—not knowing your opinions—to avoid everything of a religious kind."

"Ah! but it should be line upon line, you know; here a little, and there a little, sir. As the *bow* is bent, you know—the—hoop is made, you know, sir."

Here Mr. Appleditch stepped to the door suddenly, and peeped out, as if he feared he was wanted; but presently returning, he continued:

"But time's a precious gift, sir, and we must not waste it. So, if you'll do us the honour, sir, to dine with us next Lord's day—we may call it a work of necessity, you know—you will see the little Samuel, and—and—Mrs. Appleditch."

"I shall be very happy. What is your address, Mr. Appleditch?"

"You had better come to Salem Chapel, Dervish town, and we can go home together. Service commences at eleven. Mrs. Appleditch will be glad to see you. Ask for Mr. Appleditch's pew. Goo-ood morning, sir."

Hugh took his leave, half inclined to send an excuse before the day arrived, and decline the *connection.* But his principle was, to take whatever offered, and thus make way for the next thing. Besides, he thus avoided the responsibility of choice, from which he always shrunk.

He returned to his novel; but, alas! the inventive faculty point-blank refused to work under the weight of such a Sunday in prospect. He wandered out, quite dispirited; but, before long, to take his revenge upon circumstances, resolved at least to have a dinner out of them. So he went to a chop-house, had a chop and a glass of ale, and was astonished to find how much he enjoyed them. In fact, abstinence gave his very plain dinner more than all the charms of a feast—a fact of which Hugh has not been the only discoverer. He studied *Punch* all the time he ate, and rose with his spirits perfectly restored.

"Now I am in for it," said he, "I will be extravagant for once." So he went and bought a cigar, which he spun out into three miles of smoke, as he wandered through Shoreditch, and Houndsditch, and Petticoat-lane, gazing at the faces of his brothers and sisters; which faces having been so many years wrapt in a fog both moral and physical, now looked out of it as if they were only the condensed nuclei of the same fog and filth.

As he was returning through Whitechapel, he passed a man on the pavement, whose appearance was so remarkable that he could not help looking back after him. When he reflected about it, he thought that it must have been a certain indescribable resemblance to David Elginbrod that had so attracted him. The man was very tall. Six-foot Hugh felt dwarfed beside him; for he had to look right up, as he passed, to see his face. He was dressed in loose, shabby black. He had high and otherwise very marked features, and a dark complexion. A general carelessness of demeanour was strangely combined with an expression of reposeful strength and quiet concentration of will. At how much of this conclusion Hugh arrived after knowing more of him, I cannot tell; but such was the description he gave of him as he saw him first; and it was thoroughly correct. His countenance always seemed to me (for I knew him well) to represent a nature ever bent in one direction, but never in haste, because never in doubt.

To carry his extravagance and dissipation still further, Hugh now betook himself to the pit of the Olympic Theatre; and no one could have laughed more heartily, or cried more helplessly, that night, than he; for he gave himself wholly up to the influences of the ruler of the hour, the admirable Robson. But what was his surprise when, standing up at the close of the first act, and looking around and above him, he saw, unmistakeably, the same remarkable countenance looking down upon him from the front row of the gallery. He continued his circuit of observation, trying to discover the face of Funkelstein in the boxes or circles ; but involuntarily he turned his gaze back to the strange countenance, which still seemed bent towards his. The curtain rose, and during the second act he forgot all about everything else. At its close he glanced up to the gallery again, and there was the face still, and still looking at him. At the close of the third act it had vanished, and he saw nothing more of it that evening. When the after-piece was over, for he sat it out, he walked quietly home, much refreshed. He had needed some relaxation, after many days of close and continuous labour.

But awfully solemn was the face of good Miss Talbot, as she opened the door for him at midnight. Hugh took especial pains with his boots and the door-mat, but it was of no use: the austerity of her countenance would not relax in the least. So he took his candle and walked up-stairs to his room, saying only as he went—being unable to think of anything else:

"Good night, Miss Talbot."

But no response proceeded from the offended divinity of the place.

He went to bed, somewhat distressed at the behaviour of Miss Talbot, for he had a weakness for being on good terms with everybody. But he resolved *to have it out* with her next morning; and so fell asleep and dreamed of the strange man who had watched him at the theatre.

He rose next morning at the usual time. But his breakfast was delayed half an hour; and when it came, the maid waited upon him, and not her mistress, as usual. When he had finished, and she returned to take away the ruins, he asked her to say to her mistress that he wanted to speak to her. She brought back a message, which she delivered with some difficulty, and evidently under compulsion—that if Mr. Sutherland wanted to speak to her, he would find her in the back parlour. Hugh went down instantly, and found Miss Talbot in a doubly frozen condition, her face absolutely blue with physical and mental cold combined. She waited for him to speak. Hugh began:

"Miss Talbot, it seems something is wrong between you and me."

"Yes, Mr. Sutherland."

"Is it because I was rather late last night?"

"*Rather* late, Mr. Sutherland?"

Miss Talbot showed no excitement. With her, the thermometer, in place of rising under the influence of irritation, steadily sank.

"I cannot make myself a prisoner on parole, you know, Miss Talbot. You must leave me my liberty."

"Oh, yes, Mr. Sutherland. Take your liberty. You'll go the way of all the rest. It's no use trying to save any of you."

"But I'm not aware that I am in any particular want of saving, Miss Talbot."

"There it is!—Well, till a sinner is called and awakened, of course it's no use. So I'll just do the best I can for you. Who can tell when the Spirit may be poured from on high? But it's very sad to me, Mr. Sutherland, to see an amiable young man like you going the way of transgressors, which is hard. I am sorry for you, Mr. Sutherland."

Though the ice was not gone yet, it had begun to melt under the influences of Hugh's good-temper, and Miss Talbot's sympathy with his threatening fate. Conscience, too, had something to do with the change; for, much as one of her temperament must have disliked making such a confession, she ended by adding, after a pause:

"And very sorry, Mr. Sutherland, that I showed you any bad temper last night."

Poor Miss Talbot! Hugh saw that she was genuinely troubled about him, and resolved to offend but seldom, while he was under her roof.

"Perhaps, when you know me longer, you will find I am steadier than you think."

"Well, it may be. But steadiness won't make a Christian of you."

"It may make a tolerable lodger of me, though," answered Hugh; "and you wouldn't turn me into the street because I am steady and nothing more, would you?"

"I said I was sorry, Mr. Sutherland. Do you wish me to say more?"

"Bless your kind heart!" said Hugh. "I was only joking."

He held out his hand to Miss Talbot, and her eyes glistened as she took it. She pressed it kindly, and abandoned it instantly.

So all was right between them once more.

"Who knows," murmured Miss Talbot, "but the Lord may save him? He's surely not far from the kingdom of heaven. I'll do all I can to make him comfortable."

CHAPTER VI.

A SUNDAY'S DINNER.

Some books are lies frae end to end,
And some great lies were never penned:
Even ministers, they hae been kenned,
In holy rapture,
Great lies and nonsense baith to vend,
And nail't wi' Scripture.

BURNS.

To the great discomposure of Hugh, Sunday was incvitablc, and hc had to set out for Salem Chapel. He found it a neat little Noah's Ark of a place, built in the shape of a cathedral, and consequently sharing in the general disadvantages to which dwarfs of all kinds are subjected, absurdity included. He was shown to Mr. Appleditch's pew. That worthy man received him in sleek black clothes, with white neck-cloth, and Sunday face composed of an absurd mixture of stupidity and sanctity. He stood up, and Mrs. Appleditch stood up, and Master Appleditch stood up, and Hugh saw that the ceremony of the place required that he should force his way between the front of the pew and the person of each of the human beings occupying it, till he reached the top, where there was room for him to sit down. No other recognition was taken till after service.

Meantime the minister ascended the pulpit-stair, with all the solemnity of one of the self-elect, and a priest besides. He was just old enough for the intermittent attacks of self-importance to which all youth is exposed, to have in his case become chronic. He stood up and worshipped his creator aloud, after a manner which seemed to say in every tone: "Behold I am he that worshippeth Thee! How mighty art Thou!" Then he read the Bible in a quarrelsome sort of way, as if he were a bantam, and every verse were a crow of defiance to the sinner. Then they sang a hymn in a fashion which brought dear old Scotland to Hugh's mind, which has the sweetest songs in its cottages, and the worst singing in its churches, of any country in the world. But it was almost equalled here; the chief cause of its badness being the absence of a modest self-restraint, and consequent tempering of the tones, on the part of the singers; so that the result was what Hugh could describe only as *scraichin.**

I was once present at the worship of some being who is supposed by negroes to love drums and cymbals, and all clangorous noises. The resemblance, according to Hugh's description, could not have been a very distant one. And yet I doubt not that some thoughts of worshipping love mingled with the noise; and perhaps the harmony of these with the spheric melodies, sounded the sweeter to the angels, from the earthly discord in which they were lapped.

* *ch* guttural. The land-rail is a *corn-scraich.*

Then came the sermon. The text was the story of the good Samaritan. Some idea, if not of the sermon, yet of the value of it, may be formed from the fact, that the first thing to be considered, or, in other words, the first head was, "The culpable imprudence of the man in going from Jerusalem to Jericho without an escort."

It was in truth a strange, grotesque, and somewhat awful medley—not unlike a dance of Death, in which the painter has given here a lovely face, and there a beautiful arm or an exquisite foot, to the wild-prancing and exultant skeletons. But the parts of the sermon corresponding to the beautiful face or arm or foot, were but the fragments of Scripture, shining like gold amidst the worthless ore of the man's own production—worthless, save as gravel or chaff or husks have worth, in a world where dilution, and not always concentration, is necessary for healthfulness.

But there are Indians who eat clay, and thrive on it more or less, I suppose. The power of assimilation which a growing nature must possess is astonishing. It will find its food, its real Sunday dinner, in the midst of a whole cartload of refuse; and it will do the whole week's work on it. On no other supposition would it be possible to account for the earnest face of Miss Talbot, which Hugh espied turned up to the preacher, as if his face were the very star in the east, shining to guide the chosen kings. It was well for Hugh's power of endurance, that he had heard much the same thing in Scotland, and the same thing better dressed, and less grotesque, but more lifeless, and at heart as ill-mannered, in the church of Arnstead.

Just before concluding the service, the pastor made an announcement in the following terms: "After the close of the present service, I shall be found in the adjoining vestry by all persons desirous of communicating with me on the state of their souls, or of being admitted to the privileges of church-fellowship. Brethren, we have this treasure in earthen vessels, and so long as *this* vessel lasts"—here he struck his chest so that it resounded—"it shall be faithfully and liberally dispensed. Let us pray."

After the prayer, he spread abroad his arms and hands as if he would clasp the world in his embrace, and pronounced the benediction in a style of arrogance that the pope himself would have been ashamed of.

The service being thus concluded, the organ absolutely blasted the congregation out of the chapel, so did it storm and rave with a fervour anything but divine.

My readers must not suppose that I give this chapel as the type of orthodox dissenting chapels. I give it only as an approximate specimen of a large class of them. The religious life which these communities once possessed, still lingers in those of many country districts and small towns, but is, I fear, all but gone from those of the cities and larger towns. What of it remains in these, has its chief manifestation in the fungous growth of such chapels as the one I have described, the congregations themselves taking this for a sure indication of the prosperity of the *body*. How much even of the kind of prosperity which they ought to indicate, is in reality at the foundation of these appearances, I would recommend those to judge who are versed in the mysteries of chapel-building societies.

As to Hugh, whether it was that the whole affair was suggestive of Egyptian bondage, or that his own mood was, at the time, of the least comfortable sort, I will not pretend to determine; but he assured me that he felt all the time, as if, instead of being in a chapel built of bricks harmoniously arranged, as by the lyre of Amphion, he were wandering in the waste, wretched field whence these bricks had been dug, of all places on the earth's surface the most miserable, assailed by the nauseous odours, which have not character enough to be described, and only remind one of the colours on a snake's back.

When they reached the open air, Mr. Appleditch introduced Hugh to Mrs. Appleditch, on the steps in front of the chapel.

"This is Mr. Sutherland, Mrs. Appleditch."

Hugh lifted his hat, and Mrs. Appleditch made a courtesy. She was a very tall woman —a head beyond her husband, extremely thin, with sharp nose, hollow cheeks, and good eyes. In fact, she was partly pretty, and might have been pleasant-looking, but for a large, thin-lipped, vampire-like mouth, and a general expression of greed and contempt. She was meant for a lady, and had made herself a money-maggot. She was richly and plainly dressed; and until she began to be at her ease, might have passed for an unpleasant *lady*. Master Appleditch, the future pastor, was a fat boy, dressed like a dwarf, in a frock coat and man's hat, with a face in which the meanness and keenness strove for mastery, and between them kept down the appearance of stupidity consequent on fatness. They walked home in silence, Mr. and Mrs. Appleditch apparently pondering either upon the spiritual food they had just received, or the corporeal food for which they were about to be thankful.

Their house was one of many in a crescent. Not content with his sign in town, the grocer had a large brass plate on his door, with *Appleditch* engraved upon it in capitals: it saved them always looking at the numbers. The boy ran on before, and assailed this door with a succession of explosive knocks.

As soon as it was opened, in he rushed, bawling:

"Peter, Peter, here's the new apprentice! Papa's brought him home to dinner, because he was at chapel this morning." Then in a lower tone—"I mean to have a ride on his back this afternoon."

The father and mother laughed. A solemn priggish little voice answered:

"Oh, no, Johnny. Don't yon know what day this is? This is the Sabbath-day."

"The dear boy!" sighed his mother.

"That boy is too good to live," responded the father.

Hugh was shown into the dining-roo where the table was already laid for dinn It was evident that the Appleditches we well-to-do people. The room was full of wh is called handsome furniture, in a high state polish. Over the chimney-piece hung t portrait of a preacher in gown and bands, t most prominent of whose features were l cheeks.

In a few minutes the host and host entered, followed by a pale-faced little b the owner of the voice of reproof.

"Come here, Peetie," said his mother, "a tell Mr. Sutherland what you have got." S referred to some toy—no, not toy, for it w the Sabbath—to some book, probably.

Peetie answered in a solemn voice, mou ing every vowel:

"I've got five bags of gold in the Bank England."

"Poor child!" said his mother, with scornful giggle. "You wouldn't have mu to reckon on, if that were all."

Two or three gaily dressed riflemen passed the window. The poor fellows, unable to bear the look of their Sunday clothes, if they had any, after being used to their uniform, had come out in all its magnificence.

"Ah!" said Mr. Appleditch, "that's all very well in a state of nature; but when a man is once born into a state of grace, Mr. Sutherland—ah!"

"Really," responded Mrs. Appleditch, "the worldliness of the lower classes is quite awful. But they are spared for a day of wrath, poor things! I am sure that accident on the railway last Sabbath, might have been a warning to them all. After that they can't say there is not a God that ruleth in the earth, and taketh vengeance for his broken Sabbaths."

"Mr. ——I don't know your name," said Peter, whose age Hugh had just been trying in vain to conjecture.

"Mr. Sutherland," said the mother.

"Mr. Slubberman, are you a converted character?" resumed Peter.

"Why do you ask me that, Master Peter?" said Hugh, trying to smile.

"I think you look good, but mamma says she don't think you are, because you say Sunday instead of Sabbath, and she always finds people who do are worldly."

Mrs. Appleditch turned red—not blushed, and said, quickly:

"Peter shouldn't repeat everything he hears."

"No more I do, ma. I haven't told what you said about ——"

Here his mother caught him up, and carried him out of the room, saying:

"You naughty boy! you shall go to bed."

"Oh, no, I shan't!"

"Yes, you shall. Here, Jane, take this naughty boy to bed."

"I'll scream."

"*Will* you?"

"Yes, I will!"

> And such a yell was there
> Of sudden and portentous birth,
> As if . . . . .

ten cats were being cooked alive.

"Well! well! well! my Peetie! He shan't go to bed, if he'll be a good boy. Will he be good?"

"May I stay up to supper, then? May I?"

"Yes, yes; anything to stop such dreadful screaming. You are very naughty—very naughty *indeed.*"

"No. I'm not naughty. I'll scream again."

"No, no. Go and get your pinafore on, and come down to dinner. *Any*thing rather than a scream."

I am sick of all this, and doubt if it is worth printing; but it amused me very much one night as Hugh related it over a bottle of Chablis and a pipe.

He certainly did not represent Mrs. Appleditch in a very favourable light on the whole; but he took care to say that there was a certain liberality about the table, and a kind of heartiness in her way of pressing him to have more than he could possibly eat, which contrasted strangely with her behaviour afterwards in money matters. There are many people who can be liberal in almost anything but money. They seem to say, "Take anything but my purse." Miss Talbot told him afterwards, that this same lady was quite active amongst the poor of her district. She made it a rule never to give money, or at least never more than sixpence; but she turned scraps of victuals and cast-off clothes to the best account; and, if she did not make friends with the mammon of unrighteousness, she yet kept an eye on the eternal habitations in the distribution of the crumbs that fell from her table. Poor Mr. Appleditch, on the other hand, often embezzled a shilling or a half-crown from the till, for the use of a poor member of the same church—meaning by *church*, the individual community to which he belonged; but of this, Mrs. Appleditch was carefully kept ignorant.

After dinner was over, and the children had been sent away, which was effected without a greater amount of difficulty than, from the anticipative precautions adopted, appeared to be lawful and ordinary, Mr. Appleditch proceeded to business.

"Now, Mr. Sutherland, what do you think of Johnnie, sir?"

"It is impossible for me to say yet; but I am quite willing to teach him if you like."

"He's a forward boy," said his mother.

"Not a doubt of it," responded Hugh; for he remembered the boy asking him, across the table: "Isn't our Mr. Lixom"—(the pastor) —"a oner?"

"And very eager and retentive," said his father.

Hugh had seen the little glutton paint both cheeks to the eyes with damson tart, and render more than a quantity proportionate to the colouring, invisible.

"Yes, he is eager, and retentive, too, I daresay," he said; "but much will depend on whether he has a turn for study.

"Well, you will find that out to-morrow. I think you will be surprised, sir."

"At what hour would you like me to come?"

"Stop, Mr. Appleditch," interposed his wife. "You have said nothing yet about terms; and that is of some importance, considering the rent and taxes we pay."

"Well, my love, what do you feel inclined to give?"

"How much do you charge a lesson, Mr. Sutherland? Only let me remind you, sir, that he is a very little boy, although stout, and that you cannot expect to put much Greek and Latin into him for some time yet. Besides, we want you to come *every* day, which ought to be considered in the rate of charge."

"Of course it ought," said Hugh.

"How much do you say, then, sir?"

"I should be content with half-a-crown a lesson."

"I daresay you would!" replied the lady, with indignation. "Half-a-crown! That's —six half-crowns is—fifteen shillings. Fifteen shillings a week for that mite of a boy! Mr. Sutherland, you ought to be ashamed of yourself, sir."

"You forget, Mrs. Appleditch, that it is as much trouble to me to teach one little boy —yes, a great deal more than to teach twenty grown men."

"You ought to be ashamed of yourself, sir. You a Christian man, and talk of trouble in teaching such a little cherub as that?"

"But do pray remember the distance I have to come, and that it will take nearly four hours of my time every day."

"Then you can get lodgings nearer."

"But I could not get any so cheap."

"Then you can the better afford to do it."

And she threw herself back in her chair, as if she had struck the decisive blow. Mr. Appleditch remarked, gently:

"It is good for your health to walk the distance, sir."

Mrs. Appleditch resumed:

"I won't give a farthing more than one shilling a lesson. There, now!"

"Very well," said Hugh, rising; "then I

must wish you good day. We need not waste more time in talking about it."

"Surely you are not going to make any use of your time on a Sunday?" said the grocer, mildly. "Don't be in a hurry, Mr. Sutherland. We tradespeople like to make the best bargain we can."

"Mr. Appleditch, I am ashamed of you. You always will be vulgar. You always smell of the shop."

"Well, my dear, how can I help it? The sugar and soft-soap will smell, you know."

"Mr. Appleditch, you disgust me!"

"Dear! dear! I am sorry for that.—Suppose we say to Mr. Sutherland——"

"Now, you leave that to me. I'll tell you what, Mr. Sutherland—I'll give you eighteenpence a lesson, and your dinner on the Sabbath; that is, if you sit under Mr. Lixom in —n pew, and walk home with us."

teen shi, I must decline," said Hugh. "I Mr. Suth my Sundays for myself."

yourself, sir. ditch was disappointed. She had

coveted the additional importance which the visible possession of a live tutor would secure her at "Salem."

"Ah! Mr. Sutherland," she said. "And I must trust my child, with an immortal soul in his inside, to one who wants the Lord's only day for himself!—for *himself*, Mr. Sutherland!"

Hugh made no answer, because he had none to make. Again Mrs Appleditch resumed:

"Shall it be a bargain, Mr. Sutherland? Eighteen-pence a lesson—that's nine shillings a week—and begin to-morrow?"

Hugh's heart sunk within him, not so much with disappointment as with disgust.

But to a man who is making nothing, the prospect of earning ever so little, is irresistibly attractive. Even on a shilling a day, he could keep hunger at arm's length. And a beginning is half the battle. He resolved.

"Let it be a bargain, then, Mrs. Appleditch."

The lady immediately brightened up, and at once put on her company-manners again, behaving to him with great politeness, and a sneer that would not be hid away under it. From this Hugh suspected that she had made a better bargain than she had hoped; but the discovery was now too late, even if he could have brought himself to take advantage of it. He hated bargain-making as heartily as the grocer's wife loved it.

He very soon rose to take his leave.

"Oh!" said Mrs. Appleditch to her husband, "but Mr. Sutherland has not seen the drawing-room!"

Hugh wondered what there could be remarkable about the drawing-room; but he soon found that it was the pride of Mrs. Appleditch's heart. She abstained from all use of it except upon great occasions—when parties of her friends came to drink tea with her. She made a point, however, of showing it to everybody who entered the house for the first time. So Hugh was led up-stairs, to undergo the operation of being shown the drawing-room, and being expected to be astonished at it.

I asked him what it was like. He answered:

"It was just what it ought to be—rich and ugly. Mr. Appleditch, in his deacon's uniform, hung over the fire, and Mrs. Appleditch, in her wedding-dress, over the piano; for there was a piano, and she could play psalm-tunes on it with one finger. The round table in the middle of the room had books in gilded red and blue covers symmetrically arranged all round it. This is all I can recollect."

Having feasted his eyes on the magnificence thus discovered to him, he walked home, more depressed at the prospect of his new employment than he could have believed possible.

On his way, he turned aside into the Regent's Park, where the sight of the people enjoying themselves—for it was a fine day for the season—partially dispelled the sense of living corruption and premature burial which he had experienced all day long. He kept as far off from the rank of open-air preachers as possible, and really was able to thank God that all the world did not keep Scotch Sabbath—a day neither Mosaic, nor Jewish, nor Christian:

not Mosaic, inasmuch as it kills the very essence of the fourth commandment, which is *Rest*, transmuting it into what the chemists would call a mechanical mixture of *service* and *inertia;* not Jewish, inasmuch as it is ten times more severe, and formal, and full of negations, than that of the Sabbatarian Jews reproved by the Saviour for their idolatry of the day; and unchristian, inasmuch as it insists, beyond appeal, on the observance of times and seasons, abolished, as far as *law* is concerned, by the word of the chief of the apostles; and elevates into an especial test of piety a custom not even mentioned by the founders of christianity at all—that, namely, of accounting this day more holy than all the rest.

These last are but outside reasons for calling it unchristian. There are far deeper and more important ones, which cannot well be produced here.

It is not Hugh, however, who is to be considered accountable for all this, but the historian of his fortunes, between whom and the vision of a Lord's Day indeed, there arises too often the nightmare-memory of a Scotch Sabbath—between which and its cousin, the English Sunday, there is too much of a family likeness. The grand men and women whom I have known in Scotland, seem to me, as I look back, to move about in the mists of a Scotch Sabbath, like a company of way-worn angels in the Limbo of Vanity, in which there is no air whereupon to smite their sounding wings, that they may rise into the sunlight of God's presence.

CHAPTER VII.

SUNDAY EVENING.

Now resteth in my memory but this point, which indeed is the chief to you of all others; which is the choice of what men you are to direct yourself to; for it is certain no vessel can leave a worse taste in the liquor it contains, than a wrong teacher infects an unskilful hearer with that which hardly will ever out. . . . . But you may say, "How shall I get excellent men to take pains to speak with me?" Truly, in few words, either by much expense or much humbleness.

Letter of Sir Philip Sidney to his brother Robert.

How many things which, at the first moment, strike us as curious coincidences, afterwards become so operative on our lives, and so interwoven with the whole web of their histories, that instead of appearing any more as strange accidents, they assume the shape of unavoidable necessities, of homely, ordinary, lawful occurrences, as much in their own place as any shaft or pinion of a great machine!

It was dusk before Hugh turned his steps homeward. He wandered along, thinking of Euphra and the Count and the stolen rings. He greatly desired to clear himself to Mr. Arnold. He saw that the nature of the ring tended to justify Mr. Arnold's suspicions; for a man who would not steal for money's worth, might yet steal for value of another sort, addressing itself to some peculiar weakness; and Mr. Arnold might have met with instances of this nature in his position as magistrate. He greatly desired, likewise, for Euphra's sake, to have Funkelstein in his power. His own ring was beyond recovery; but if, by its means, he could hold such a lash over him as would terrify him from again exercising his villainous influences on her, he would be satisfied.

While plunged in this contemplation, he

came upon two policemen talking together. He recognized one of them as a Scotchman, from his speech. It occurred to him at once to ask his advice, in a modified manner; and a moment's reflection convinced him that it would at least do no harm. He would do it. It was one of those resolutions at which one arrives by an arrow flight of the intellect.

"You are a countryman of mine, I think," said he, as soon as the two had parted.

"If ye're a Scotchman, sir—may be ay, may be no."

"Whaur come ye frae, man?"

"Ou, Aberdeen-awa."

"It's mine ain calf-country. An' what do they ca' ye?"

"They ca' me John MacPherson."

"My name's Sutherland."

"Eh, man! It's my ain mither's name. Gie's a grup o' yer han', Maister Sutherlan'.—Eh, man!" he repeated, shaking Hugh's hand with vehemence.

"I have no doubt," said Hugh, relapsing into

English, "that we are some cousins or other. It's very lucky for me to find a relative, for I wanted some—advice."

He took care to say *advice*, which a Scotchman is generally prepared to bestow of his best. Had it been *sixpence*, the cousinship would have required elaborate proof, before the treaty could have made further progress.

"I'm fully at your service, sir."

"When will you be off duty?"

"At nine o'clock preceesely."

"Come to number 13, —— Square, and ask for me. It's not far."

"Wi' pleesir, sir, 'gin 'twar twise as far."

Hugh would not have ventured to ask him to his house on Sunday night, when no refreshments could be procured, had he not remembered a small *pig* (*Anglicé* stone bottle) of real mountain dew, which he had carried with him when he went to Arnstead, and which had lain unopened in one of his boxes.

Miss Talbot received her lodger with more show of pleasure than usual, for he came lapped in the odour of the deacon's sanctity. But she was considerably alarmed and beyond measure shocked when the policeman called and requested to see him. Sally had rushed in to her mistress in dismay.

"Please 'm, there's a pleaceman wants Mr. Sutherland. Oh! lor'm!"

"Well, go and let Mr. Sutherland know, you stupid girl," answered her mistress, trembling.

"Oh! lor 'm!" was all Sally's reply, as she vanished to bear the awful tidings to Hugh.

"He can't have been housebreaking already," said Miss Talbot to herself, as she confessed afterwards. "But it may be forgery or embezzlement. I told the poor deluded young man that the way of transgressors was hard."

"Please, sir, you're wanted, sir," said Sally, out of breath, and pale as her Sunday apron.

"Who wants me?" asked Hugh.

"Please, sir, the pleaceman, sir," answered Sally, and burst into tears.

Hugh was perfectly bewildered by the

girl's behaviour, and said in a tone of surprise:

"Well, show him up, then."

"Ooh! sir," said Sally, with a Plutonic sigh, and began to undo the hooks of her dress; "if you wouldn't mind, sir, just put on my frock and apron, and take a jug in your hand, an' the pleaceman 'll never look at you. I'll take care of everything till you come back, sir." And again she burst into tears.

Sally was a great reader of the *Family Herald*, and knew that this was an orthodox plan of rescuing a prisoner. The kindness of her anxiety moderated the expression of Hugh's amusement; and having convinced her that he was in no danger, he easily prevailed upon her to bring the policeman upstairs.

Over a tumbler of toddy, the weaker ingredients of which were procured by Sally's glad connivance, with a lingering idea of propitiation, and a gentle hint that *Missus mustn't know*—the two Scotchmen, seated at opposite corners of the fire, had a long chat. They began about the old country, and the places and people they both knew, and both didn't know. If they had met on the shores of the central lake of Africa, they could scarcely have been more *couthy* together. At length Hugh referred to the object of his application to MacPherson.

"What plan would you have me pursue, John, to get hold of a man in London?"

"I could manage that for ye, sir. I ken maist the haill mengie o' the detaictives."

"But you see, unfortunately, I don't wish, for particular reasons, that the police should have anything to do with it."

"Ay! ay! Hm! Hm! I see brawly. Ye'll be efter a stray sheep, nae doot?"

Hugh did not reply; so leaving him to form any conclusion he pleased.

"Ye see," MacPherson continued, "it's no that easy to a body that's no up to the trade. Hae ye ony clue like, to set ye spierin' upo'?"

"Not the least."

The man pondered a while.

"I hae't," he exclaimed at last. "What a

le I was no to think o' that afore! Gin't be a
air bit yow-lammie like, 'at ye're efter, I'll
ll ye what: there's ae man, a countryman
our ain, an' a gentleman forbye, that'll do
air for ye in that way, nor a' the detaictives
egither; an' that's Robert Falconer, Esquire.
I ken him weel."

"But I don't," said Hugh.

"But I'll introduce ye till 'im. He bides
ose at han' here; roun' twa corners jist.
n' I'm thinkin' he'll be at hame the noo; for
saw him gaein that get, afore ye cam' up to
e. An' the suner we gang, the better; for
e's no aye to be gotten haud o'. Fegs! he
ay be in Shoreditch or this."

"But will he not consider it an intrusion?"

"Na, na; there's no fear o' that. He's ony
an's an' ilka woman's freen—so be he can do
em a guid turn; but he's no for drinkin'
id daffin' an' that. Come awa', Maister
itherlan', he's yer verra man."

Thus urged, Hugh rose and accompanied
e policeman. He took him round rather

more than two corners; but within five minutes they stood at Mr. Falconer's door. John rang. The door opened without visible service, and they ascended to the first floor, which was inclosed something after the Scotch fashion. Here a respectable looking woman awaited their ascent.

"Is Mr. Falconer at hom', mem?" said Hugh's guide.

"He is; but I think he's just going out again."

"Will ye tell him, mem, 'at hoo John MacPherson, the policeman, would like sair to see him?"

"I will," she answered; and went in, leaving them at the door.

She returned in a moment, and, inviting them to enter, ushered them into a large bare room, in which there was just light enough for Hugh to recognize, to his astonishment, the unmistakeable figure of the man whom he had met in Whitechapel, and whom he had afterwards seen apparently watching him from the gallery of the Olympic Theatre.

"How are you, MacPherson?" said a deep powerful voice, out of the gloom.

"Verra weel, I thank ye, Mr. Falconer. Hoo are ye yersel', sir?"

"Very well too, thank you. Who is with you?"

"It's a gentleman, sir, by the name o' Mr. Sutherlan', wha wants your help, sir, aboot somebody or ither 'at he's enteresstit in, wha's disappeared."

Falconer advanced, and, bowing to Hugh, said, very graciously:

"I shall be most happy to serve Mr. Sutherland, if in my power. Our friend MacPherson has rather too exalted an idea of my capabilities, however."

"Weel, Maister Falconer, I only jist spier at yersel', whether or no ye was ever dung wi' onything ye took in han'."

Falconer made no reply to this. There was the story of a whole life in his silence—past and to come.

He merely said:

"You can leave the gentleman with me, then, John. I'll take care of him."

"No fear o' that, sir. Deil a bit! though a' the policemen i' Lonnon war efter 'im."

"I'm much obliged to you for bringing him."

"The obligation's mine, sir—an' the gentleman's. Good nicht, sir. Good nicht, Mr. Sutherlan'. Ye'll ken whaur to fin' me gin ye want me. Yon's my beat for anither fortnicht."

"And you know my quarters," said Hugh, shaking him by the hand. "I am greatly obliged to you."

"Not a bit, sir. Or gin ye war, ye sud be hertily welcome."

"Bring candles, Mrs. Ashton," Falconer called from the door. Then, turning to Hugh, "Sit down, Mr. Sutherland," he said, "if you can find a chair that is not illegally occupied already. Perhaps we had better wait for the candles. What a pleasant day we have had!"

"Then you have been more pleasantly occupied than I have," thought Hugh, to whose mind returned the images of the Appleditch family and its drawing-room, followed by the anticipation of the distasteful duties of the morrow. But he only said:

"It has been a most pleasant day."

"I spent it strangely," said Falconer.

Here the candles were brought in.

The two men looked at each other full in the face. Hugh saw that he had not been in error. The same remarkable countenance was before him. Falconer smiled.

"We have met before," said he.

"We have," said Hugh.

"I had a conviction we should be better acquainted, but I did not expect it so soon."

"Arc you a *clairvoyant*, then?"

"Not in the least."

"Or, perhaps, being a Scotchman, you have the second sight?"

"I am hardly Celt enough for that. But I am a sort of a seer, after all—from an instinct of the spiritual relations of things, I hope; not in the least from the nervo-material side."

"I think I understand you."

"Are you at leisure?"

"Entirely."

"Had we not better walk, then? I have to go as far as Somers Town—no great way; and we can talk as well walking as sitting."

"With pleasure," answered Hugh, rising.

"Will you take anything before you go? A glass of port? It is the only wine I happen to have."

"Not a drop, thank you. I seldom taste anything stronger than water."

"I like that. But I like a glass of port too. Come then."

And Falconer rose—and a great rising it was; for, as I have said, he was two or three inches taller than Hugh, and much broader across the shoulders; and Hugh was no stripling now. He could not help thinking again of his old friend, David Elginbrod, to whom he had to look up to find the living eyes of him, just as now he looked up to find Falconer's. But there was a great difference between those organs in the two men. David's had been of an ordinary size, pure keen blue, sparkling out of cerulean depths of peace and hope, full of lambent gleams when he was loving any one, and ever ready to be dimmed with the mists of rising emotion. All that Hugh could yet discover of Falconer's eyes was, that they were large, and black as night, and set so far back in his head, that each gleamed out of its caverned arch like the reversed torch of the Greek Genius of Death, just before going out in night. Either the frontal sinus was very large, or his observant faculties were peculiarly developed.

They went out, and walked for some distance in silence. Hugh ventured to say at length:

"You said you had spent the day strangely: may I ask how?"

"In a condemned cell in Newgate," answered Falconer. "I am not in the habit of going to such places, but the man wanted to see me, and I went."

As Falconer said no more, and as Hugh was afraid of showing anything like vulgar curiosity, this thread of conversation broke. Nothing worth recording passed until they entered a narrow court in Somers Town.

"Are you afraid of infection?" Falconer said.

"Not in the least, if there be any reason for exposing myself to it."

"That is right.—And I need not ask if you are in good health."

"I am in perfect health."

"Then I need not mind asking you to wait for me till I come out of this house. There is typhus in it."

"I will wait with pleasure. I will go with you if I can be of any use."

"There is no occasion. It is not your business this time."

So saying, Falconer opened the door, and walked in.

Said Hugh to himself: "I must tell this man the whole story; and with it all my own."

In a few minutes Falconer rejoined him, looking solemn, but with a kind of relieved expression on his face.

"The poor fellow is gone," said he.

"Ah!"

"What a thing it must be, Mr. Sutherland, for a man to break out of the choke-damp of a typhus fever into the clear air of the life beyond!"

"Yes," said Hugh; adding, after a slight hesitation, "if he be at all prepared for the change."

"Where a change belongs to the natural order of things," said Falconer, "and arrives inevitably at some hour, there must always be more or less preparedness for it. Besides, I think a man is generally prepared for a breath of fresh air."

Hugh did not reply, for he felt that he did not fully comprehend his new acquaintance. But he had a strong suspicion that it was because he moved in a higher region than himself.

"If you will still accompany me," resumed Falconer, who had not yet adverted to Hugh's object in seeking his acquaintance, "you will, I think, be soon compelled to believe that, at whatever time death may arrive, or in whatever condition the man may be at the time, it comes as the best and only good that can at that moment reach him. We are, perhaps, too much in the habit of thinking of death as the culmination of disease, which, regarded only in itself, is an evil, and a terrible evil. But I think rather of death as the first pulse of the new strength, shaking itself free from the old mouldy remnants of earth-garments, that it may begin in freedom the new life that grows out of the old. The caterpillar dies into the butterfly. Who knows but disease may be the coming, the keener life, breaking into this, and beginning to destroy like fire the inferior modes or garments of the present? And then disease would be but the sign of the salvation of fire; of the agony of the greater life to lift us to itself, out of that wherein we are failing and sinning. And so we praise the consuming fire of life."

"But surely all cannot fare alike in the new life."

"Far from it. According to the condition.

But what would be hell to one, will be quietness, and hope, and progress to another; because he has left worse behind him, and in this the life asserts itself, and is.—But perhaps you are not interested in such subjects, Mr. Sutherland, and I weary you."

"If I have not been interested in them hitherto, I am ready to become so now. Let me go with you."

"With pleasure."

As I have attempted to tell a great deal about Robert Falconer and his pursuits elsewhere, I will not here relate the particulars of their walk through some of the most wretched parts of London. Suffice it to say that, if Hugh, as he walked home, was not yet prepared to receive and understand the half of what Falconer had said about death, and had not yet that faith in God that gives as perfect a peace for the future of our brothers and sisters, who, alas! have as yet been fed with husks, as for that of ourselves, who have eaten bread of the finest of the wheat, and have been but a little thankful,—he yet felt at least that it was a blessed thing that these men and women would all die—must all die. That spectre from which men shrink, as if it would take from them the last shivering remnant of existence, he turned to for some consolation even for them. He was prepared to believe that they could not be going to worse in the end, though some of the rich and respectable and educated might have to receive their evil things first in the other world; and he was ready to understand that great saying of Schiller—full of a faith evident enough to him who can look far enough into the saying:

"Death cannot be an evil, for it is universal."

CHAPTER VIII.

EUPHRA.

Samson. O that torment should not be confined
To the body's wounds and sores,
. . . .
But must secret passage find
To the inmost mind.
. . . .
Dire inflammation, which no cooling herb
Or medicinal liquor can asswage,
Nor breath of vernal air from snowy Alp.
Sleep hath forsook and given me o'er
To death's benumming opium as my only cure,
Thence faintings, swoonings of despair,
And sense of heaven's desertion.

MILTON.—*Samson Agonistes.*

HITHERTO I have chiefly followed the history of my hero, if *hero* in any sense he can yet be called. Now I must leave him for a while, and take up the story of the rest of the few persons concerned in my tale.

Lady Emily had gone to Madeira, and Mr. Arnold had followed. Mrs. Elton and Harry, and Margaret, of course, had gone to London. Euphra was left alone at Arnstead.

A great alteration had taken place in this strange girl. The servants were positively afraid of her now, from the butler down to the kitchen-maid. She used to go into violent fits of passion, in which the mere flash of her eyes was overpowering. These outbreaks would be followed almost instantaneously by seasons of the deepest dejection, in which she would confine herself to her room for hours, or, lame as she was, wander about the house and the Ghost's Walk, herself pale as a ghost, and looking meagre and wretched.

Also, she became subject to frequent fainting-fits, the first of which took place the night before Hugh's departure, after she had returned to the house from her interview with him in the Ghost's Walk. She was evidently miserable.

For this misery we know that there were very sufficient reasons, without taking into account the fact that she had no one to fascinate now. Her continued lameness, which her restlessness aggravated, likewise gave her great cause for anxiety. But I presume that, even during the early part of her confinement, her mind had been thrown back upon itself, in that consciousness which often arises in loneliness and suffering; and that even then she had begun to feel that her own self was a worse tyrant than the count, and made her a more wretched slave than any exercise of his unlawful power could make her.

Some natures will endure an immense amount of misery before they feel compelled to look there for help, whence all help and healing comes. They cannot believe that there is verily an unseen mysterious power, till the world and all that is in it has vanished in the smoke of despair; till cause and effect is nothing to the intellect, and possible glories have faded from the imagination; then, deprived of all that made life pleasant or hopeful, the immortal essence, lonely and wretched and unable to cease, looks up with its now unfettered and wakened instinct, to the source of its own life—to the possible God who, notwithstanding all the improbabilities of his existence, may yet perhaps be, and may yet perhaps hear his wretched creature that calls. In this loneliness of despair, life must find The Life; for joy is gone, and life is all that is left: it is compelled to seek its source, its root, its eternal life. This alone remains as a possible thing. Strange condition of despair into which the Spirit of God drives a man—a condition in which the Best alone is the Possible!

Other simpler natures look up at once. Even before the first pang has passed away, as by a holy instinct of celestial childhood, they lift their eyes to the heavens whence cometh their aid. Of this class Euphra was not. She belonged to the former. And yet even she had begun to look upward, for the waters had closed above her head. She betook herself to the one man of whom she had heard as knowing about God. She wrote, but no answer came. Days and days passed away, and there was no reply.

"Ah! just so!" she said, in bitterness. "And if I cried to God for ever, I should hear no word of reply. If he be, he sits apart, and leaves the weak to be the prey of the bad. What cares he?"

Yet, as she spoke, she rose, and, by a sudden impulse, threw herself on the floor, and cried for the first time:

"O God, help me!"

Was there voice or hearing?

She rose at least with a little hope, and with the feeling that if she could cry to him, it might be that he could listen to her. It seemed natural to pray; it seemed to come of itself: that could not be except it was first natural for God to hear. The foundation of her own action must be in him who made her; for her call could be only a response after all.

The time passed wearily by. Dim, slow

November days came on, with the fall of the last brown shred of those clouds of living green that had floated betwixt earth and heaven. Through the bare boughs of the overarching avenue of the Ghost's Walk, themselves living skeletons, she could now look straight up to the blue sky, which had been there all the time. And she had begun to look up to a higher heaven, through the bare skeleton shapes of life; for the foliage of joy had wholly vanished—shall we say in order that the children of the spring might come?—certainly in order first that the blue sky of a deeper peace might reflect itself in the hitherto darkened waters of her soul.

Perhaps some of my readers may think that she had enough to repent of to keep her from weariness. She had plenty to repent of, no doubt; but repentance, between the paroxysms of its bitterness, is a very dreary and November-like state of the spiritual weather. For its foggy mornings and cheerless noons cannot believe in the sun of spring, soon to ripen into the sun of summer; and its best time is the night, that shuts out the world and weeps its fill of slow tears. But she was not altogether so blameworthy as she may have appeared. Her affectations had not been altogether false. She valued, and in a measure possessed, the feelings for which she sought credit. She had a genuine enjoyment of nature, though after a sensuous, Keats-like fashion, not a Wordsworthian. It was the body, rather than the soul, of nature that she loved—its beauty rather than its truth. Had her love of nature been of the deepest, she would have turned aside to conceal her emotions rather than have held them up as allurements in the eyes of her companion. But as no body and no beauty can exist without soul and truth, she who loves thc former must at least be capable of loving the deeper essence to which they owe their very existence.

This view of her character is borne out by her love of music and her liking for Hugh. Both were genuine. Had the latter been either more or less genuine than it was, the task of fascination would have been more difficult, and its success less complete. Whether her own feelings became further involved than she had calculated upon, I cannot tell; but surely it says something for her, in any case, that she desired to retain Hugh as her friend, instead of hating him because he *had been* her lover.

How glad she would have been of Harry now! The days crawled one after the other like weary snakes. She tried to read the New Testament: it was to her like a mouldy chamber of worm-eaten parchments, whose windows had not been opened to the sun or the wind for centuries; and in which the dust of the decaying leaves choked the few beams that found their way through the age-blinded panes.

This state of things could not have lasted long; for Euphra would have died. It lasted, however, until she felt that she had been leading a false, worthless life; that she had been casting from her every day the few remaining fragments of truth and reality that yet kept her nature from falling in a heap of helpless ruin; that she had never been a true friend to any one; that she was of no value—fit for no one's admiration, no one's love. She must leave her former self, like a dead body, behind her, and rise into a purer air of life and reality, else she would perish with that everlasting death which is the disease and corruption of the soul itself.

To those who know anything of such experiences, it will not be surprising that such feelings as these should be alternated with fierce bursts of passion. The old self then started up with feverish energy, and writhed for life. Never any one tried to be better, without, for a time, seeming to himself, perhaps to others, to be worse. For the suffering of the spirit weakens the brain itself, and the whole physical nature groans under it; while the energy spent in the effort to awake, and arise from the dust, leaves the regions previously guarded by prudence naked to the wild inroads of the sudden destroying impulses born of suffering, self-sickness, and hatred. As in the delirious patient, they would dash to the earth whatever comes first within reach, as if the thing first perceived, and so (by perception alone) brought into contact with the suffering, were the cause of all the distress.

One day a letter arrived for her. She had had no letter from any one for weeks. Yet, when she saw the direction, she flung it from her. It was from Mrs. Elton, whom she disliked, because she found her utterly uninteresting and very stupid.

Poor Mrs. Elton laid no claim to the contraries of these epithets. But in proportion as she abjured thought, she claimed speech, both by word of mouth and by letter. Why not? There was nothing in it. She considered reason as an awful enemy to the soul, and obnoxious to God, especially when applied to find out what he means when he addresses us as reasonable creatures. But speech? There was no harm in that. Perhaps it was some latent conviction that this power of speech was the chief distinction between herself and the lower animals, that made her use it so freely, and at the same time open her purse so liberally to the Hospital for Orphan Dogs and Cats. Had it not been for her own dire necessity, the fact that Mrs. Elton was religious would have been enough to convince Euphra that there could not possibly be anything in religion.

The letter lay unopened till next day—a fact easy to account for, improbable as it may seem; for besides writing as largely as she talked, and less amusingly because more correctly, Mrs. Elton wrote such an indistinct though punctiliously neat hand, that the reading of a letter of hers involved no small amount of labour. But the sun shining out next morning, Euphra took courage to read it, while drinking her coffee, although she could not expect to make that ceremony more pleasant thereby. It contained an invitation to visit Mrs. Elton at her house in —— Street, Hyde Park, with the assurance that, now that everything was arranged, they had plenty of room for her. Mrs. Elton was sure she must be lonely at Arnstead; and Mrs. Horton could, no doubt, be trusted—and so on.

Had this letter arrived a few weeks earlier, Euphra would have infused into her answer a skilful concoction of delicate contempt; not for the amusement of knowing that Mrs. Elton would never discover a trace of it, but simply for a relief to her own dislike. Now she would have written a plain letter, containing as brief and as true an excuse as she could find, had it not been that, inclosed in Mrs. Elton's note she found another, which ran thus:

"DEAR EUPHRA,—Do come and see us. I do not like London at all without you. There are no happy days here like those we had at Arnstead with Mr. Sutherland. Mrs. Elton and Margaret are very kind to me. But I wish you would come. Do, do, do. Please do.

"Your affectionate cousin,

"HARRY ARNOLD."

"The dear boy!" said Euphra, with a gush of pure and grateful affection; "I will go and see *him*."

Harry had begun to work with his masters, and was doing his best, which was very good. If his heart was not so much in it as when he was studying with his big brother, he gained a great benefit from the increase of exercise to his will, in the doing of what was less pleasant. Ever since Hugh had given his faculties a right direction, and aided him by healthful manly sympathy, he had been making up for the period during which childhood had been protracted into boyhood; and now he was making rapid progress.

When Euphra arrived, Harry rushed to the hall to meet her. She took him in her arms, and burst into tears. Her tears drew forth his. He stroked her pale face, and said:

"Dear Euphra, how ill you look!"

"I shall soon be better now, Harry."

"I was afraid you did not love me, Euphra; but now I am sure you do."

"Indeed I do. I am very sorry for everything that made you think I did not love you."

"No, no. It was all my fancy. Now we shall be very happy."

And so Harry was. And Euphra, through means of Harry, began to gain a little of what is better than most kinds of happiness, because it is nearest to the best happiness—I mean *peace*. This foretaste of rest came to her from the devotedness with which she now applied herself to aid the intellect, which she had unconsciously repressed and stunted before. She took Harry's books when he had gone to bed; and read over all his lessons, that she might be able to assist him in preparing them; venturing thus into some regions of labour into which ladies are too seldom conducted by those who instruct them. This produced in her quite new experiences. One of these was, that in proportion as she laboured for Harry, hope grew for herself. It was likewise of the greatest immediate benefit that the intervals of thought, instead of lying vacant to melancholy, or the vapours that sprung from the foregoing strife of the spiritual elements, should be occupied by healthy mental exercise.

Still, however, she was subject to great vicissitudes of feeling. A kind of peevishness, to which she had formerly been a stranger, was but too ready to appear, even when she was most anxious, in her converse with Harry, to behave well to him. But the pure forgiveness of the boy was wonderful. Instead of plaguing himself to find out the cause of her behaviour, or resenting it in the least, he only laboured, by increased attention and submission, to remove it; and seemed perfectly satisfied when it was followed by a kind word, which to him was repentance, apology, amends, and betterment, all in one. When he had thus driven away the evil spirit, there was Euphra her own self. So perfectly did she see, and so thoroughly appreciate this kindness and love of Harry, that he began to look to her like an angel of forgiveness come to live a boy's life, that he might do an angel's work.

Her health continued very poor. She suffered constantly from more or less headache, and at times from faintings. But she had not for some time discovered any signs of somnambulism.

Of this peculiarity her friends were entirely ignorant. The occasions, indeed, on which it had manifested itself to an excessive degree, had been but few.

CHAPTER IX.

THE NEW PUPILS.

Think you a little din can daunt mine ears?
Have I not in my time heard lions roar?
. . . .
And do you tell me of a woman's tongue,
That gives not half so great a blow to hear,
As will a chestnut in a farmer's fire?
Tush! tush! fear boys with bugs.

Taming of the Shrew.

DURING the whole of his first interview with Falconer, which lasted so long that he had been glad to make a bed of Falconer's sofa, Hugh never once referred to the object for which he had accepted MacPherson's proffered introduction; nor did Falconer ask him any questions. Hugh was too much interested and saddened by the scenes through which Falconer led him, not to shrink from speaking of anything less important; and with Falconer it was a rule, a principle almost, never to expedite utterance of any sort.

In the morning, feeling a little good-natured anxiety as to his landlady's reception of him, Hugh made some allusion to it, as he sat at his new friend's breakfast-table.

Falconer said:

"What is your landlady's name?"

"Miss Talbot."

"Oh! little Miss Talbot? You are in good quarters—too good to lose, I can tell you. Just say to Miss Talbot that you were with me."

"You know her, then?"

"Oh, yes."

"You seem to know everybody."

"If I have spoken to a person once, I never forget him."

"That seems to me very strange."

"It is simple enough. The secret of it is, that, as far as I can help it, I never have any merely business relations with any one. I try always not to forget that there is a deeper relation between us. I commonly succeed worst in a drawing-room; yet even there, for the time we are together, I try to recognize the present humanity, however much distorted or concealed. The consequence is, I never forget anybody; and I generally find that others remember me—at least those with whom I have had any real relations, springing from my need or from theirs. The man who mends a broken chair for you, or a rent in your coat, renders you a human service; and, in virtue of that, comes nearer to your inner self, than nine-tenths of the ladies and gentlemen whom you meet only in what is called society, are likely to do."

"But do you not find it awkward sometimes?"

"Not in the least. I am never ashamed of knowing any one; and as I never assume a familiarity that does not exist, I never find it assumed towards me."

Hugh found the advantage of Falconer's

sociology when he mentioned to Miss Talbot that he had been his guest that night.

"You should have sent us word, Mr. Sutherland," was all Miss Talbot's reply.

"I could not do so before you must have been all in bed. I was sorry, but I could hardly help it."

Miss Talbot turned away into the kitchen. The only other indication of her feeling in the matter was, that she sent him up a cup of delicious chocolate for his lunch, before he set out for Mr. Appleditch's, where she had heard at the shop that he was going.

My reader must not be left to fear that I am about to give a detailed account of Hugh's plans with these unpleasant little immortals, whose earthly nature sprang from a pair whose religion consisted chiefly in negations, and whose main duty seemed to be to make money in small sums, and spend it in smaller. When he arrived at Buccleuch Crescent, he was shown into the dining-room, into which the boys were separately dragged, to receive the first instalment of the mental legacy left them by their ancestors. But the legacy-duty was so heavy that they would gladly have declined paying it, even with the loss of the legacy itself; and Hugh was dismayed at the impossibility of interesting them in anything. He tried telling them stories even, without success. They stared at him, it is true; but whether there was more speculation in the open mouths, or in the fishy, overfed eyes, he found it impossible to determine. He could not help feeling the riddle of Providence in regard to the birth of these, much harder to read than that involved in the case of some of the little thieves whose acquaintance he had made, when with Falconer, the evening before. But he did his best; and before the time had expired—two hours, namely,—he had found out, to his satisfaction, that the elder had a turn for sums, and the younger for drawing. So he made use of these predilections to bribe them to the exercise of their intellect upon less-favoured branches of human accomplishment. He found the plan operate as well as it could have been expected to operate upon such material.

But one or two little incidents, relating to his intercourse with Mrs. Appleditch, I must not omit. Though a mother's love is more ready to purify itself than most other loves—yet there is a class of mothers, whose love is only an extended, scarcely an expanded, selfishness. Mrs. Appleditch did not in the least love her children because they were children, and children committed to her care by the Father of all children; but she loved them dearly because they were *her* children.

One day Hugh gave Master Appleditch a smart slap across the fingers, as the ultimate resource. The child screamed as he well knew how. His mother burst into the room.

"Johnny, hold your tongue!"

"Teacher's been and hurt me."

"Hold your tongue, I say. My head's like to split. Get out of the room, you little ruffian!"

She seized him by the shoulders, and turned

him out, administering a box on his ear that made the room ring. Then turning to Hugh,

"Mr. Sutherland, how *dare* you strike my child?" she demanded.

"He required it, Mrs. Appleditch. I did him no harm. He will mind what I say another time."

"I will not have him touched. It's disgraceful. To strike a child!"

She belonged to that class of humane parents who consider it cruel to inflict any corporal suffering upon children, except they do it themselves, and in a passion. Johnnie behaved better after this, however; and the only revenge Mrs. Appleditch took for this interference with the dignity of her eldest born, and, consequently, with her own as his mother, was, that—with the view, probably, of impressing upon Hugh a due sense of the menial position he occupied in her family—she always paid him his fee of one shilling and sixpence every day before he left the house. Once or twice she contrived accidentally that the sixpence should be in coppers. Hugh was too much of a philosopher, however, to mind this from such a woman. I am afraid he rather enjoyed her spite; for he felt it did not touch him, seeing it could not be less honourable to be paid by the day than by the quarter or by the year. Certainly the coppers were an annoyance; but if the coppers could be carried, the annoyance could be borne. The real disgust in the affair was, that he had to meet and speak with a woman every day, for whom he could feel nothing but contempt and aversion. Hugh was not yet able to mingle with these feelings any of the leaven of that charity which they need most of all who are contemptible in the eyes of their fellows. Contempt is murder committed by the intellect, as hatred is murder committed by the heart. Charity having life in itself, is the opposite and destroyer of contempt as well as of hatred.

After this, nothing went amiss for some time. But it was very dreary work to teach such boys—for the younger came in for the odd sixpence. Slow, stupid resistance appeared to be the only principle of their behaviour towards him. They scorned the man whom their mother despised and valued for the self-same reason, namely, that he was cheap. They would have defied him had they dared, but he managed to establish an authority over them—and to increase it. Still, he could not rouse them to any real interest in their studies. Indeed, they were as near being little beasts as it was possible for children to be. Their eyes grew dull at a story-book, but greedily bright at the sight of bulls' eyes or toffee. It was the same day after day, till he was sick of it. No doubt they made some progress, but it was scarcely perceptiblc to him. Through fog and fair, through frost and snow, through wind and rain, he trudged to that wretched house. No one minds the weather—no young Scotchman, at least—where any pleasure waits the close of the struggle: to fight his way to misery was more than he could well endure. But his deliverance was nearer than he expected. It was not to come just yet, however.

All went on with frightful sameness, till sundry doubtful symptoms of an alteration in the personal appearance of Hugh having accumulated at last into a mass of evidence, forced the conviction upon the mind of the grocer's wife, that her tutor was actually growing a beard. Could she believe her eyes? She said she could not. But she acted on their testimony notwithstanding; and one day suddenly addressing Hugh, said, in her usual cold, thin, cutting fashion of speech:

"Mr. Sutherland, I am astonished and grieved that you, a teacher of babes, who should set an example to them, should disguise yourself in such an outlandish figure."

"What do you mean, Mrs. Appleditch?" asked Hugh, who, though he had made up his mind to follow the example of Falconer, yet felt uncomfortable enough, during the transition period, to know quite well what she meant.

"What do I mean, sir? It is a shame for a man to let his beard grow like a monkey."

"But a monkey hasn't a beard," retorted Hugh, laughing. "Man is the only animal who has one."

This assertion, if not quite correct, was approximately so, and went much nearer the truth than Mrs. Appleditch's argument.

"It's no joking matter, Mr. Sutherland, with my two darlings growing up to be ministers of the gospel."

"What! both of them?" thought Hugh. "Good heavens!" But he said:

"Well, but you know, Mrs. Appleditch, the Apostles themselves wore beards."

"Yes, when they were Jews. But who would have believed them if they had preached the gospel like old clothesmen? No, no, Mr. Sutherland, I see through all that. My own uncle was a preacher of the word. —As soon as the Apostles became Christians, they shaved. It was the sign of Christianity.

The Apostle Paul himself says that cleanliness is next to godliness."

Hugh restrained his laughter, and shifted his ground.

"But there is nothing dirty about them," he said.

"Not dirty? Now really, Mr. Sutherland, you provoke me. Nothing dirty in long hair all round your mouth, and going into it every spoonful you take?"

"But it can be kept properly trimmed, you know."

"But who's to trust you to do that? No, no, Mr. Sutherland; you must *not* make a guy of yourself."

Hugh laughed, and said nothing. Of course his beard would go on growing, for he could not help it.

So did Mrs. Appleditch's wrath.

CHAPTER X.

CONSULTATIONS.

Wo keine Götter sind, walten Gespenster.

NOVALIS.—*Die Christenheit.*

Where gods are not, spectres rule.

Ein Charakter ist ein vollkommen gebildeter Wille.

NOVALIS.—*Moralische Ansichten.*

A character is a perfectly formed will.

It was not long before Hugh repeated his visit to Falconer. He was not at home. He went again and again, but still failed in finding him. The day after the third failure, however, he received a note from Falconer, mentioning an hour at which he would be at home on the following evening. Hugh went. Falconer was waiting for him.

"I am very sorry. I am out so much," said Falconer.

"I ought to have taken the opportunity when I had it," replied Hugh. "I want to ask your help. May I begin at the beginning, and tell you all the story? or must I epitomize and curtail it?"

"Be as diffuse as you please. I shall understand the thing the better."

So Hugh began, and told the whole of his history, in as far as it bore upon the story of the crystal. He ended with the words:

"I trust, Mr. Falconer, you will not think that it is from a love of talking that I have said so much about this affair."

"Certainly not. It is a remarkable story. I will think what can be done. Meantime I will keep my eyes and ears open. I may find the fellow. Tell me what he is like."

Hugh gave as minute a description of the count as he could.

"I think I see the man," said Falconer. "I am pretty sure I shall recognise him."

"Have you any idea what he could want with the ring?"

"It is one of the curious coincidences which are always happening," answered Falconer, "that a newspaper of this very day would have enabled me, without any previous knowledge of similar facts, to give a probably correct suggestion as to his object. But you can judge for yourself."

So saying, Falconer went to a side-table, heaped up with books and papers, maps, and instruments of various kinds, apparently in triumphant confusion. Without a moment's hesitation, notwithstanding, he selected the paper he wanted, and handed it to Hugh, who read in it a letter to the editor, of which the following is a portion:—

"I have for over thirty years been in the habit of investigating the question by means of crystals. And since 18—, I have possessed the celebrated crystal, once belonging to Lady Blessington, in which very many persons, both children and adults, have seen visions of the spirits of the deceased, or of beings claiming to be such, and of numerous angels and other beings of the spiritual world. These have in all cases supported the purest and most liberal Christianity. The faculty of seeing in the crystal I have found to exist in about one person in ten among adults, and in nearly nine in every ten among children; many of whom appear to lose the faculty as they grow to adult age, unless they practise it continually."

"Is it possible," said Hugh, pausing, "that this can be a veritable paper of to-day? *Are* there people to believe such things."

"There are more fools in the world, Mr. Sutherland, than there are crystals in its mountains."

Hugh resumed his reading. He came at length to this passage:

"The spirits—which I feel certain they are—which appear, do not hesitate to inform us on all possible subjects which may tend to improve our morals, and confirm our faith in the Christian doctrines. . . . . The character they give of the class of spirits who are in the habit of communicating with mortals by rapping and such proceedings, is such that it behoves all Christian people to be on their guard against error and delusion through their means."

Hugh had read this passage aloud.

"Is not that a comfort, now, Mr. Sutherland?" said Falconer. "For in all the reports which I have seen of the religious instruction communicated in that highly articulate manner, Calvinism, high and low, has predominated. I strongly suspect the crystal phantoms of Arminianism, though. Fancy the old disputes of infant Christendom perpetuated amongst the paltry ghosts of another realm!"

"But," said Hugh, "I do not quite see how this is to help me, as to the count's object in securing the ring; for certainly, however deficient he may be in such knowledge, he is not likely to have committed the theft for the sake of instruction in the doctrines of the sects."

"No. But such a crystal might be put to

other, not to say better, uses. Besides, Lady Blessington's crystal might be a pious crystal; and the other which belonged to Lady ——"

"Lady Euphrasia."

"To Lady Euphrasia, might be a worldly crystal altogether. This might reveal demons and their counsels, while that was haunted by theological angels and evangelical ghosts."

"Ah! I see. I should have thought, however, that the count had been too much of a man of the world to believe such things."

"He might find his account in it, notwithstanding. But no amount of world-wisdom can set a man above the inroads of superstition. In fact, there is but one thing that can free a man from superstition, and that is belief. All history proves it. The most sceptical have ever been the most credulous. This is one of the best arguments for the existence of something to believe."

"You remind me of a passage in my story which I omitted, as irrelevant to the matter in hand."

"Do let me have it. It cannot fail to interest me."

Hugh gave a complete account of the experiments they had made with the careering plate. Now the writing of the name of *David Elginbrod* was the most remarkable phenomenon of the whole, and Hugh was compelled, in responding to the natural interest of Falconer, to give a description of David. This led to a sketch of his own sojourn at Turriepuffit; in which the character of David came out far more plainly than it could have come out in any description. When he had finished, Falconer broke out, as if he had been hitherto restraining his wrath with difficulty:

"And that was the man the creatures dared to personate! I hate the whole thing, Sutherland. It is full of impudence and irreverence. Perhaps the wretched beings may want another thousand years' damnation, because of the injury done to their character by the homage of men who ought to know better."

"I do not quite understand you."

"I mean, that you ought to believe as easily that such a man as you describe is laughing with the devil and his angels, as that he wrote a copy at the order of a charlatan, or worse."

"But it could hardly be deception."

"Not deception? A man like him could not get through them without being recognized."

"I don't understand you. By whom?"

"By swarms of low miserable creatures that so lament the loss of their beggarly bodies that they would brood upon them in the shape of flesh-flies, rather than forsake the putrifying remnants. After that, chair or table or anything that they can come into contact with, possesses quite sufficient organization for such. Don't you remember that once, rather than have no body to go into, they crept into the very swine? There was a fine passion for self-embodiment and sympathy! But the swine themselves could not stand it, and preferred drowning."

"Then you do think there was something supernatural in it?"

"Nothing in the least. It required no supernatural powers to be aware that a great man was dead, and that you had known him well. It annoys me, Sutherland, that able men, ay, and good men too, should consult with ghosts whose only possible superiority consists in their being out of the body. Why should they be the wiser for that? I should as soon expect to gain wisdom by taking off my clothes, and to lose it by getting into bed; or to rise into the seventh heaven of spirituality by having my hair cut. An impudent forgery of that good man's name! If I were you, Sutherland, I would have nothing to do with such a low set. They are the canaille of the other world. It's of no use to lay hold on their skirts, for they can't fly. They're just like the vultures—easy to catch, because they're full of garbage. I doubt if they have more intellect left than just enough to lie with.—I have been compelled to think a good deal about these things of late."

Falconer put a good many questions to Hugh, about Euphra and her relation to the count; and such was the confidence with which he had inspired him, that Hugh felt at perfect liberty to answer them all fully, not avoiding even the exposure of his own feelings, where that was involved by the story.

"Now," said Falconer, "I have material out of which to construct a theory. The count is at present like a law of nature concerning which a prudent question is the first half of the answer, as Lord Bacon says; and you can put no question without having first formed a theory, however slight or temporary; for otherwise no question will suggest itself. But, in the meantime, as I said before, I will make inquiry upon the theory that he is somewhere in London, although I doubt it."

"Then I will not occupy your time any longer at present," said Hugh. "Could you say, without fettering yourself in the least, when I might be able to see you again?"

"Let me see. I will make an appointment

with you.—Next Sunday; here; at ten o'clock in the morning. Make a note of it."

"There is no fear of my forgetting it. My consolations are not so numerous that I can afford to forget my sole pleasure. You, I should think, have more need to make a note of it than I, though I am quite willing to be forgotten, if necessary."

"I never forget my engagements," said Falconer.

They parted, and Hugh went home to his novel.

CHAPTER XI.

QUESTIONS AND DREAMS.

On a certain time the Lady St. Mary had commanded the Lord Jesus to fetch her some water out of the well. And when he had gone to fetch the water, the pitcher, when it was brought up full, brake. But Jesus, spreading his mantle, gathered up the water again, and brought it in that to his mother.—*The First (apocryphal) Gospel of the* INFANCY *of* JESUS CHRIST.

MRS. ELTON read prayers morning and evening; —very elaborate compositions, which would have instructed the apostles themselves in many things they had never anticipated. But, unfortunately, Mrs. Elton must likewise read certain remarks, in the form of a homily, intended to impress the scripture which preceded it upon the minds of the listeners.

Between the mortar of the homilist's faith, and the dull blows of the pestle of his arrogance, the fair form of truth was ground into the powder of pious small talk. This result was not pleasant either to Harry or to Euphra. Euphra, with her life threatening to go to ruin about her, was crying out for him who made the soul of man, "who loved us into being," * and who alone can renew the life of his children; and in such words as those a scoffing demon seemed to mock at her needs. Harry had the natural dislike of all childlike natures to everything formal, exclusive, and unjust. But, having received nothing of what is commonly called *a religious training*, this advantage resulted from his new experiences in Mrs. Elton's family, that a good direction was given to his thoughts by the dislike which he felt to such utterances. More than this: a horror fell upon him lest these things should be true; lest the mighty *All* of nature should be only a mechanism,

* Goldsmith; twice, in the *Citizen of the World.*

without expression and without beauty; lest the God who made us should be like us only in this, that he too was selfish and mean and proud; lest his ideas should resemble those that inhabit the brain of a retired money-maker, or of an arbitrary monarch claiming a divine right—instead of towering, as the heavens over the earth, above the loftiest moods of highest poet, most generous child, or most devoted mother. I do not mean that these thoughts took these shapes in Harry's mind; but that his feelings were such as might have been condensed into such thoughts, had his intellect been more mature.

One morning, the passage of scripture which Mrs. Elton read was the story of the young man who came to Jesus, and went away sorrowful, because the Lord thought so well of him, and loved him so heartily, that he wanted to set him free from his riches. A great portion of the homily was occupied with proving that the evangelist could not possibly mean that Jesus *loved* the young man in any pregnant sense of the word; but merely meant that Jesus "felt kindly disposed towards him"—felt a poor little human interest in him, in fact, and did not love him divinely at all.

Harry's face was in a flame all the time she was reading. When the service was over —and a bond service it was for Euphra and him—they left the room together. As soon as the door was shut, he burst out:

"I say, Euphra! Wasn't that a shame? They would have Jesus as bad as themselves. We shall have somebody writing a book next to prove that after all Jesus was a Pharisee."

"Never mind," said the heart-sore, sceptical Euphra; "never mind, Harry; it's all nonsense."

"No, it's not all nonsense. Jesus *did* love the young man. I believe the story itself before all the Doctors of Divinity in the world. He loves all of us, he does—with all his heart, too."

"I hope so," was all she could reply; but she was comforted by Harry's vehement confession of faith.

Euphra was so far softened, or perhaps weakened, by suffering, that she yielded many things which would have seemed impossible before. One of these was that she went to church with Mrs. Elton, where that lady hoped she would get good to her soul. Harry of course was not left behind. The church she *frequented* was a fashionable one, with a vicar more fashionable still; for had he left that church, more than half his congregation, which consisted mostly of ladies, would have left it also, and followed him to the ends of London. He was a middle-aged man, with a rubicund countenance, and a gentle familiarity of manner, that was exceedingly pleasing to the fashionable sheep who, conscious that they had wandered from the fold, were waiting with exemplary patience for the barouches and mail-phaetons of the skies to carry them back without the trouble of walking. Alas for them! they have to learn that the chariots of heaven are chariots of fire.

The Sunday morning following the conversation I have just recorded, the clergyman's sermon was devoted to the illustration of the greatness and condescension of the Saviour. After a certain amount of tame excitement expended upon the consideration of his power and kingdom, one passage was wound up in this fashion:

"Yes, my friends, even her most gracious Majesty, Queen Victoria, the ruler over millions diverse in speech and in hue, to whom we all look up with humble submission, and whom we acknowledge as our sovereign lady—even she, great as she is, adds by her homage a jewel to his crown; and, hailing him as her Lord, bows and renders him worship! Yet this is he who comes down to visit, yea, dwells with his own elect, his chosen ones, whom he has led back to the fold of his grace."

For some reason, known to himself, Falconer had taken Hugh, who had gone to him according to appointment that morning, to this same church. As they came out, Hugh said:

"Mr. —— is quite proud of the honour done his master by the queen."

"I do not think," answered Falconer, "that his master will think so much of it; for he once had his feet washed by a woman that was a sinner."

The homily which Mrs. Elton read at prayers that evening, bore upon the same subject nominally as the chapter that preceded it—that of election; a doctrine which in the Bible asserts the fact of God's choosing certain persons for the specific purpose of receiving first, and so communicating the gifts of his grace to the whole world; but which, in the homily referred to, was taken to mean the choice of certain persons for ultimate salvation, to the exclusion of the rest. They were sitting in silence after the close, when Harry started up suddenly, saying: "I don't want God to love me, if he does not love everybody;" and, bursting into tears, hurried out of the room. Mrs. Elton was awfully shocked at his wickedness. Euphra hastened after him; but he would not return, and went supperless to bed. Euphra, however, carried him some supper. He sat up in bed and ate it with the tears in his eyes. She kissed him, and bade him good night; when, just as she was leaving the room, he broke out with:

"But only think, Euphra, if it should be true! I would rather not have been made."

"It is *not* true," said Euphra, in whom a faint glimmer of faith in God awoke for the sake of the boy whom she loved—awoke to comfort him, when it would not open its eyes for herself. "No, Harry dear, if there is a God at all, he is not like that."

"No, he can't be," said Harry vehemently, and with the brightness of a sudden thought; "for if he were like that, he wouldn't be a God worth being; and that couldn't be, you know."

Euphra knelt by her bedside, and prayed more hopefully than for many days before. She prayed that God would let her know that he was not an idol of man's invention.

Till friendly sleep came, and untied the knot of care, both Euphra and Harry lay troubled with things too great for them. Even in their sleep, the care would gather again, and body itself into dreams. The first thought that visited Harry when he awoke, was the memory of his dream: that he died and went to heaven; that heaven was a great church just like the one Mrs. Elton went to, only larger; that the pews were filled with angels, so crowded together that they had to tuck up their wings very close indeed—and Harry could not help wondering what they wanted them for; that they were all singing psalms; that the pulpit by a little change had been converted into a throne, on which sat God the Father, looking very solemn and severe; that Jesus was seated in the reading-desk, looking very sad; and that the Holy Ghost sat on the clerk's desk, in the shape of a white dove; that a cherub, whose face reminded him very much of a policeman he knew, took him by the shoulder for trying to pluck a splendid green feather out of an archangel's wing, and led him up to the throne, where God shook his head at him in such a dreadful way, that he was terrified, and then stretched out his hand to lay hold on him; that he shrieked with fear; and that Jesus put out his hand and lifted him into the reading-desk, and hid him down below. And there Harry lay, feeling so safe, stroking and kissing the feet that had been weary and wounded for him, till, in the growing delight of the thought that he actually held those feet, he came awake and remembered it all. Truly it was a childish dream, but not without its own significance. For surely the only refuge from heathenish representations of God under Christian forms, the only refuge from man's blinding and paralysing theories, from the dead wooden shapes substituted for the living forms of human love and hope and aspiration, from the interpretations which render Scripture as dry as a speech in Chancery—surely the one refuge from all these awful evils is the Son of man; for no misrepresentation and no misconception can destroy the beauty of that face which the marring of sorrow has elevated into the region of reality, beyond the marring of irreverent speculation and scholastic definition. From the God of man's painting, we turn to the man of God's being, and he leads us to the true God, the radiation of whose glory we first see in him. Happy is that man who has a glimpse of this, even in a dream such as Harry's!—a dream in other respects childish and incongruous, but not more absurd than the instruction whence it sprung.

But the troubles returned with the day. Prayers revived them. He sought Euphra in her room.

"They say I must repent and be sorry for my sins," said he. "I have been trying very hard; but I can't think of any, except once that I gave Gog" (his Welch pony) "such a beating because he *would* go where I didn't want him. But he's forgotten it long ago; and I gave him two feeds of corn after it, and so somehow I can't feel very sorry now. What *shall* I do?—But that's not what I mind most. It always seems to me it would be so much grander of God to say: 'Come along, never mind. *I'll* make you good. I can't wait till you *are* good; I love you so much.'"

His own words were too much for Harry, and he burst into tears at the thought of God being so kind. Euphra, instead of trying to comfort him, cried too. Thus they continued for some time, Harry with his head on her knees, and she kindly fondling it with her distressed hands. Harry was the first to recover; for his was the April time, when rain clears the heavens. All at once he sprung to his feet, and exclaimed:

"Only think, Euphra! What if, after all, I should find out that God is as kind as you are!"

How Euphra's heart smote her!

"Dear Harry," answered she, "God must be a great deal kinder than I am. I have not been kind to you at all."

"Don't say that, Euphra. I shall be quite content if God is as kind as you."

"Oh, Harry! I hope God is like what I dreamed about my mother last night."

"Tell me what you dreamed about her, dear Euphra."

"I dreamed that I was a little child——"

"Were you a little girl when your mother died?"

"Oh, yes; such a tiny! But I can just remember her."

"Tell me your dream, then."

"I dreamed that I was a little girl, out all alone on a wild mountain-moor, tripping and stumbling on my night-gown. And the wind was so cold! And, somehow or other, the wind was an enemy to me, and it followed and caught me, and whirled and tossed me about, and then ran away again. Then I hastened on, and the thorns went into my feet, and the stones cut them. And I heard the blood from them trickling down the hill-side as I walked."

"Then they would be like the feet I saw in my dream last night."

"Whose feet were they?"

"Jesus' feet."

"Tell me about it."

"You must finish yours first, please, Euphra."

So Euphra went on:

"I got dreadfully lame. And the wind ran after me, and caught me again, and took me in his great blue ghostly arms, and shook me about, and then dropped me again to go on. But it was very hard to go on, and I couldn't stop; and there was no use in stopping, for the wind was everywhere in a moment. Then suddenly I saw before me a great cataract, all in white, falling flash from a precipice; and I thought with myself, 'I will go into the cataract, and it will beat my life out, and then the wind will not get me any more.' So I hastened towards it, but the wind caught me many times before I got near it. At last I reached it, and threw myself down into the basin it had hollowed out of the rocks. But as I was falling, something caught me gently, and held me fast, and it was not the wind. I opened my eyes, and behold! I was in my mother's arms, and she was clasping me to her breast; for what I had taken for a cataract falling into a gulf, was only my mother, with her white grave-clothes floating all about her, standing up in her grave, to look after me. "It was time you came home, my darling," she said, and stooped down into her grave with me in her arms. And oh! I was so happy; and her bosom was not cold, or her arms hard, and she carried me just like a baby. And when she stooped down, then a door opened, somewhere in the grave, I could not find out where exactly—and in a moment after, we were sitting together in a summer grove, with the tree-tops steeped in sunshine, and waving about in a quiet loving wind—oh, how different from the one that chased me home!—and we underneath in the shadow of the trees. And then I said, 'Mother, I've hurt my feet.'"

"Did you call her *mother* when you were a little girl?" interposed Harry.

"No," answered Euphra. "I called her

mamma, like other children; but in my dreams I always call her *mother*."

"And what did she say?"

"She said—'Poor child!'—and held my feet to her bosom; and after that, when I looked at them, the bleeding was all gone, and I was not lame any more."

Euphra paused with a sigh.

"Oh, Harry! I do not like to be lame."

"What more?" said Harry, intent only on the dream.

"Oh! then I was so happy, that I woke up directly."

"What a pity! But if it should come true?"

"How could it come true, dear Harry?"

"Why, this world is sometimes cold, and the road is hard—you know what I mean, Euphra."

"Yes, I do."

"I wish I could dream dreams like that! How clever you must be!"

"But you dream dreams, too, Harry. Tell me yours."

"Oh, no, I never dream dreams; the dreams dream me," answered Harry, with a smile.

Then he told his dream, to which Euphra listened with an interest uninjured by the grotesqueness of its fancy. Each interpreted the other's with reverence.

They ceased talking; and sat silent for a while. Then Harry, putting his arms round Euphra's neck, and his lips close to her ear, whispered:

"Perhaps God will say *my darling* to you some day, Euphra; just as your mother did in your dream."

She was silent. Harry looked round into her face, and saw that the tears were flowing fast.

At that instant, a gentle knock came to the door. Euphra could not reply to it. It was repeated. After another moment's delay, the door opened, and Margaret walked in.

CHAPTER XII.

A SUNDAY WITH FALCONER.

How happy is he born and taught,
  That serveth not another's will;
Whose armour is his honest thought,
  And simple truth his utmost skill.

. . . . .

This man is freed from servile bands
  Of hope to rise or fear to fall:
Lord of himself, though not of lands,
  And, having nothing, yet hath all.

SIR HENRY WOTTON.

IT was not often that Falconer went to church; but he seemed to have some design in going oftener than usual at present. The Sunday after the one last mentioned, he went as well, though not to the same church, and calling for Hugh took him with him. What they found there, and the conversation following thereupon, I will try to relate, because, although they do not immediately affect my outward story, they greatly influenced Hugh's real history.

They heard the Morning Service and the Litany read in an ordinary manner, though somewhat more devoutly than usual. Then, from the communion-table, rose a voice vibrating with solemn emotion, like the voice of Abraham pleading for Sodom. It thrilled through Hugh's heart. The sermon which followed affected him no less, although, when he came out, he confessed to Falconer that he had only caught flying glimpses of its meaning, scope, and drift.

"I seldom go to church," said Falconer; "but when I do, I come here; and always feel that I am in the presence of one of the holy servants of God's great temple not made with hands. I heartily trust that man. He is what he seems to be."

"They say he is awfully heterodox."

"They do."

"How then can he remain in the church, if he is as honest as you say?"

"In this way, as I humbly venture to think," Falconer answered. "He looks upon the formulæ of the church as utterances of *living* truth —vital embodiments—to be regarded as one ought to regard human faces. In these human faces, others may see this or that inferior expression, may find out the mean and the small and the incomplete: he looks for and finds the ideal; the grand, sacred, God-meant meaning; and by that he holds as *the* meaning of the human countenances, for it is the meaning of him who made them. So with the confession of the Church of England: he believes that not man only, but God also, and God first and chief, had to do with the making of it; and therefore he looks in it for the Eternal and the Divine, and he finds what he seeks. And as no words can avoid bearing in them the possibility of a variety of interpretations, he would exclude whatever the words might mean, or, regarded merely as words, do mean, in a narrow exposition: he thinks it would be dishonest to take the low meaning as *the* meaning. To return to the faces: he passes by moods and tempers, and beholds the main character —that on whose surface the temporal and transient floats. Both in faces and in formulæ he loves the divine substance, with his true, manly, brave heart; and as for the faults in both—for man, too, has his share in both—I believe he is ready to die by them, if only in so doing he might die for them.—I had a vision of him this morning as I sat and listened to his voice, which always seems to me to come immediately from his heart, as if his heart spoke with lips of its own. Shall I tell you my vision?—

"I saw a crowd—priests and laymen—speeding, hurrying, darting away, up a steep, crumbling height. Mitres, hoods, and hats rolled behind them to the bottom. Every one for himself, with hands and feet they scramble and flee, to save their souls from the fires of hell which come rolling in along the hollow below with the forward 'pointing spires' of billowy flame. But beneath, right in the course of the fire, stands one man upon a little rock which goes down to the centre of the great world, and faces the approaching flames. He stands bareheaded, his eyes bright with faith in God, and the mighty mouth that utters his truth, fixed in holy defiance. His denial comes from no fear, or weak dislike to that which is painful. On neither side will he tell lies for peace. He is ready to be lost for his fellow-men. In the name of God he rebukes the flames of hell. The fugitives pause on the top, look back, call him *lying prophet*, and shout evil opprobrious names at the man who counts not his own life dear to him, who has forgotten his own soul in his sacred devotion to men, who fills up what is left behind of the sufferings of Christ, for his body's sake—for the human race, of which he is the head. Be sure that, come what may of the rest, let the flames of hell ebb or flow, that man is safe, for he is delivered already from the only devil that can make hell itself a torture, the devil of selfishness—the only one that can *possess* a man and make himself his own living hell. He is out of all that region of things, and already dwelling in the secret place of the Almighty."

"Go on, go on."

"He trusts in God so absolutely, that he leaves his salvation to him—utterly, fearlessly; and, forgetting it, as being no concern of his, sets himself to do the work that God has given him to do, even as his Lord did before him, counting that alone worthy of his care. Let God's will be done, and all is well. If God's will be done, he cannot fare ill. To him, God is all in all. If it be possible to separate such things, it is the glory of God, even more than the salvation of men, that he seeks. He will not have it that his Father in heaven is not perfect. He believes entirely that God loves, yea, *is* love; and, therefore, that hell itself must be subservient to that love, and but an embodiment of it; that the grand work of Justice is to make way for a Love which will give to every man that which is right and ten times more, even if it should be by means of awful suffering—a suffering which the Love of the Father will not shun, either for himself or his children, but will eagerly meet for their sakes, that he may give them all that is in his heart."

"Surely you speak your own opinions in describing thus warmly the faith of the preacher."

"I do. He is accountable for nothing I say. All I assert is, that this is how I seem to myself to succeed in understanding him."

"How is it that so many good people call him heterodox?"

"I do not mind that. I am annoyed only when good-hearted people, with small natures and cultivated intellects, patronize him, and talk forgivingly of his warm heart and unsound judgment. To these, theology must be like a map—with plenty of lines in it. They cannot trust their house on the high table-land of his theology, because they cannot see the outlines bounding the said table-land. It is not small enough for them. They cannot take it in. Such can hardly be satisfied with the creation, one would think, seeing there is no line of division anywhere in it. They would take care there should be no mistake."

"Does God draw no lines, then?"

"When he does, they are pure lines, without breadth, and consequently invisible to mortal eyes; not Chinese walls of separation, such as these definers would construct. Such minds are *à priori* incapable of theorizing upon his theories. Or, to alter the figure, they will discover a thousand faults in his drawing, but they can never behold the figure constructed by his lines, and containing the faults which they believe they discover."

"But can those theories in religion be correct which are so hard to see?"

"They are only hard to certain natures."

"But those natures are above the average."

"Yes, in intellect and its cultivation—nothing more."

"You have granted them heart."

"Not much; but what there is, good."

"That is allowing a great deal, though. Is it not hard then to say that such cannot understand him?"

"Why? They will get to heaven, which is all they want. And they will understand him one day, which is more than they pray for. Till they have done being anxious about their own salvation, we must forgive them that they can contemplate with calmness the damnation of a universe, and believe that God is yet more indifferent than they."

"But do they not bring the charge likewise against you, of being unable to understand them?"

"Yes. And so it must remain, till the Spirit of God decide the matter, which I presume must take place by slow degrees. For this decision can only consist in the enlightenment of souls to see the truth; and therefore has to do with individuals only. There is no triumph for the Truth but that. She knows no glorying over the vanquished, for in her victory the vanquished is already of the vanquishers. Till then, the Right must be content to be called the Wrong, and—which is far harder—to seem the Wrong. There is no spiritual victory gained by a verbal conquest; or by any kind of torture, even should the rack employed be that of the purest logic. Nay more: so long as the wicked themselves remain impenitent, there is mourning in heaven; and when there is no longer any hope over one last remaining sinner, heaven itself must confess its defeat, heap upon that sinner what plagues you will."

Hugh pondered, and continued pondering till they reached Falconer's chambers. At the door Hugh paused.

"Will you not come in?"

"I fear I shall become troublesome."

"No fear of that. I promise to get rid of you as soon as I find you so."

"Thank you. Just let me know when you have had enough of me."

They entered. Mrs. Ashton, who, unlike her class, was never missing when wanted, got them some bread and cheese; and Falconer's Fortunatus-purse of a cellar—the bottom of his cupboard—supplied its usual bottle of port; to which fare the friends sat down.

The conversation, like a bird descending in spirals, settled at last upon the subject which had more or less occupied Hugh's thoughts ever since his unsatisfactory conversation with Funkelstein, at their first meeting; and still more since he had learned that this man himself exercised an unlawful influence over Euphra. He begged Falconer, if he had any theory comprehending such things, to let him know what kind of a relation it was, in which Miss Cameron stood to Funkelstein, or Count von Halkar.

"I have had occasion to think a good deal about those things," said Falconer. "The first thing evident is, that Miss Cameron is peculiarly constituted, belonging to a class which is, however, larger than is commonly supposed, circumstances rarely combining to bring out its peculiarities. In those who constitute this class, the nervous element, either from preponderating, or from not being in healthy and harmonious combination with the more material element, manifests itself beyond its ordinary sphere of operation, and so occasions results unlike the usual phenomena of life, though, of course, in accordance with natural laws. To use a simile: it is, in such cases, as if all the nerves of the human body came crowding to the surface, and there exposed themselves to a thousand influences, from which they would otherwise be preserved. Of course I am not attempting to explain, only to suggest a conceivable hypothesis. Upon such constitutions, it would not be surprising that certain other constitutions, similar, yet differing, should exercise a peculiar influence. You are, I daresay, more or less familiar with the main features of mesmerism and its allies, among which is what is called biology. I presume it is on such constitutions as I have supposed, that those powers are chiefly operative. Miss Cameron has, at some time or other in her history, submitted herself to the influences of this Count Halkar; and he has thus gained a most dangerous authority over her, which he has exercised for his own ends."

"She more than implied as much in the last conversation I had with her."

"So his *will* became her *law*. There is in the world of mind a something corresponding to physical force in the material world.—I cannot avoid just touching upon a higher analogy. The kingdom of heaven is not come, even when God's will is our law: it is come when God's will is our will. While God's will is our law, we are but a kind of noble slaves; when his will is our will, we are free children. Nothing in nature is free enough to be a symbol for the state of those who act immediately from the essence of their hidden life, and the recognition of God's will as that essence. But, as I said, this belongs to a far higher region. I only wanted to touch on the relation of the freedoms—physical, mental, and spiritual. To return to the point in hand: I recognise in the story a clear evidence of strife and partial victory in the affair of the the ring. The count—we will call him by the name he gives himself—had evidently been anxious for years to possess himself of this ring: the probable reasons we have already talked of. He had laid his injunctions on his slave to find it for him; and she, perhaps at first nothing loath, perhaps loving the man as well as submitting to him, had for a long time attempted to find it, but had failed. The count, probably doubting her sincerity, and hoping, at all events, to urge her search, followed her to Arnstead, where it is very likely he had been before, although he had avoided Mr. Arnold. Judging it advantageous to get into the house, in order to make observations, he employed his chance meeting with you to that result. But, before this, he had watched Miss Cameron's familiarity with you—was jealous and tyrannical. Hence the variations of her conduct to you; for when his power was upon her, she could not do as she pleased. But she must have had a real regard for you; for she evidently refused to get you into trouble by taking the ring from your custody. But my surprise is that the fellow limited himself to that one jewel."

"You may soon be relieved from that surprise," answered Hugh: "he took a valuable diamond of mine as well."

"The rascal! We may catch him, but you are not likely to find your diamond again. Still, there is some possibility."

"How do you know she was not willing to take it from me?"

"Because, by her own account, he had to destroy her power of volition entirely, before he could make her do it. He threw her into a mesmeric sleep."

"I should like to understand his power over her a little better. In such cases of biology—how they came to abuse the word, I should like to know——"

"Just as they call *table-rapping*, &c., *spiritualism.*"

"I suppose his relation to her must be classed amongst phenomena of that sort?"

"Certainly."

"Well, tell me, does the influence outlast the mesmeric condition?"

"If by mesmeric condition you mean any state evidently approaching to that of sleep—undoubtedly. It is, in many cases, quite independent of such a condition. Perhaps the degree of willing submission at first, may have something to do with it. But mesmeric influence, whatever it may mean, is entirely independent of sleep. That is an accident accompanying it, perhaps sometimes indicating its culmination."

"Does the person so influenced act with or against his will?"

"That is a most difficult question, involving others equally difficult. My own impression is, that the patient—for patient in a very serious sense he is—acts with his inclination, and often with his will; but in many cases with his inclination against his will. This is a very important distinction in morals, but often overlooked. When a man is acting *with* his inclination, his will is in abeyance. In our present imperfect condition, it seems to me that the absolute will has no opportunity of *pure* action, of operating entirely as itself, except when working in opposition to inclination. But to return: the power of the biologist appears to me to lie in this—he is able, by some mysterious sympathy, to produce in the mind of the patient such forceful impulses to do whatever he wills, that they are in fact irresistible to almost all who are obnoxious to his influence. The will requires an especial training and a distinct developement, before it is capable of acting with any degree of freedom. The men who have undergone this are very few indeed; and no one whose will is not educated *as will*, can, if subjected to the influences of biology, resist the impulses roused in his passive brain by the active brain of the operator. This at least is my impression.

Other things no doubt combined to increase the influence in the present case. She liked him, perhaps more than liked him once. She was partially committed to his schemes; and she was easily mesmerised. It would seem, besides, that she was naturally disposedto somnambulism. This is a remarkable co-existence of distinct developements of the same peculiarity. In this latter condition, even if in others she were able to resist him, she would be quite helpless; for all the thoughts that passed through her brain would owe their origin to his.—Imagine being forced to think another man's thoughts! That would be *possession* indeed! And this is not far removed from the old stories about the demons entering into a man.—He would be ruler over the whole intellectual life that passed in her during the time; and which to her, as far as the ideas suggested belonged to the outward world, would appear an outer life, passing all round her, not in her.

She would, in fact, be a creature of his imagination for the time, as much as any character invented, and sent through varied circumstances, feelings, and actions, by the mind of the poet or novelist. Look at the facts. She warned you to beware of the count that night before you went into the haunted bed-chamber. Even when she entered it, by your own account——"

"Entered it? Then you *do* think it was Euphra who personated the ghost?"

"I am sure of it. She was sleep-walking."

"But so different—such a death-like look!"

"All that was easy enough to manage. She refused to obey him at first. He mesmerized her. It very likely went farther than he expected; and he succeeded too well. Experienced, no doubt, in disguises, he dressed her as like the dead Lady Euphrasia as he could, following her picture. Perhaps she possessed such a disguise, and had used it before. He thus protected her from suspicion, and himself from implication.—What was the colour of the hair in the picture?

"Golden."

"Hence the sparkle of gold dust in her hair. The count managed it all. He willed that she should go, and she went. Her disguise was certain safety, should she be seen. You would suspect the ghost and no one else if she appeared to you, and you lost the ring after. But even in this state she yielded against her better inclination, for she was weeping when you saw her. But she could not help it. While you lay on the couch in the haunted chamber, where he carried you, the awful death-ghost was busy in your room, was opening your desk, fingering your papers, and stealing your ring. It is rather a frightful idea."

"She did not take my ring, I am sure. He followed her, and took it.—But she could not have come in at either door——"

"Could not? Did she not go out at one of them? Besides, I do not doubt that such a room as that had private communication with the open air as well. I should much like to examine the place."

"But how could she have gone through the bolted door then?"

"That door may have been set in another, larger by half the frame or so, and opening with a spring and concealed hinges. There is no difficulty about that. There are such places to be found now and then in old houses. But, indeed, if you will excuse me, I do not consider your testimony, on every minute particular, quite satisfactory."

"Why?" asked Hugh, rather offended.

"First, because of the state of excitement you must have been in; and next, because I doubt the wine that was left in your room. The count no doubt knew enough of drugs to put a few ghostly horrors into the decanter. But poor Miss Cameron! The horrors he has put into her mind and life! It is a sad fate—all but a sentence of insanity."

Hugh sprang to his feet.

"By heaven!" he cried, "I will strangle the knave."

"Stop, stop!" said Falconer. "No revenge! Leave him to the sleeping divinity within him, which will awake one day, and complete the hell that he is now building for himself—for the very fire of hell is the divine in it. Your work is to set Euphra free. If you did strangle him, how do you know if that would free her from him?"

"Horrible!—Have you no news of him?"

"None whatever."

"What, then, can I do for her?"

"You must teach her to foil him."

"How am I to do that? Even if I knew how, I cannot see her, I cannot speak to her."

"I have a great faith in opportunity."

"But how should she foil him?"

"She must pray to God to redeem her fettered will—to strengthen her will to redeem herself. She must resist the count, should he again claim her submission (as, for her sake, I hope he will), as she would the devil himself. She *must* overcome. Then she will be free—not before. This will be very hard to do. His power has been excessive and peculiar, and her submission long and complete. Even if he left her alone, she would not therefore be free. She must defy him; break his bonds; oppose his will; assert her freedom; and defeat him utterly."

"Oh! who will help her? I have no power. Even if I were with her, I could not help her in such a struggle. I wish David were not dead. He was the man.—*You* could now, Mr. Falconer."

"No. Except I knew her, had known her for some time, and had a strong hold of all her nature, I could not, would not try to help her. If Providence brought this about, I would do my best; but otherwise I would not interfere. But if she pray to God, he will give her whatever help she needs, and in the best way, too."

"I think it would be some comfort to her if we could find the ring—the crystal, I mean."

"It would be more, I think, if we could find the diamond."

"How can we find either?"

"We must find the count first. I have not given that up, of course. I will tell you what I should like to do, if I knew the lady."

"What?"

"Get her to come to London, and make herself as public as possible: go to operas and balls, and theatres; be presented at court; take a stall at every bazaar, and sell charity puff-balls—get as much into the papers as possible. 'The lovely, accomplished, fascinating Miss Cameron, &c., &c.'"

"What do you mean?"

"I will tell you what I mean. The count has forsaken her now; but as soon as he heard that she was somebody, that she was followed and admired, his vanity would be roused, his old sense of property in her would revive, and he would begin once more to draw her into his toils. What the result would be, it is impossible to foretell; but it would at least give us a chance of catching him, and her a chance of resisting him."

"I don't think, however, that she would

venture on that course herself. I should not dare to propose it to her."

"No, no. It was only an invention, to deceive myself with the fancy that I was doing something. There would be many objections to such a plan, even if it were practicable. I must still try to find him, and if fresh endeavours should fail, devise fresher still."

"Thank you a thousand times," said Hugh. "It is too good of you to take so much trouble."

"It is my business," answered Falconer. "Is there not a soul in trouble?"

Hugh went home, full of his new friend. With the clue he had given him, he was able to follow all the windings of Euphra's behaviour, and to account for almost everything that had taken place. It was quite painful to him to feel that he could be of no immediate service to her; but he could hardly doubt that, before long, Falconer would, in his wisdom and experience, excogitate some mode of procedure in which he might be able to take a part.

He sat down to his novel, which had been making but little progress for some time; for it is hard to write a novel when one is living in the midst of a romance. But the romance, at this time, was not very close to him. It had a past and a possible future, but no present. That same future, however, might at at any moment dawn into the present.

In the meantime, teaching the Latin grammar and the English alphabet to young aspirants after the honours of *the ministry*, was not work inimical to invention, from either the exhaustion of its excitement or the absorption of its interest.

CHAPTER XIII.

THE LADY'S-MAID.

Her yellow hair, beyond compare,
  Comes trinkling down her swan-white neck;
And her two eyes, like stars in skies,
  Would keep a sinking ship frae wreck.
Oh! Mally's meek, Mally's sweet,
  Mally's modest and discreet;
Mally's rare, Mally's fair,
  Mally's every way complete.

BURNS.

What arms for innocence but innocence.

GILES FLETCHER.

MARGARET had sought Euphra's room, with the intention of restoring to her the letter which she had written to David Elginbrod. Janet had let it lie for some time before she sent it to Margaret; and Euphra had given up all expectation of an answer.

Hopes of ministration filled Margaret's heart;

but she expected, from what she knew of her, that anger would be Miss Cameron's first feeling. Therefore, when she heard no answer to her application for admission, and had concluded, in consequence, that Euphra was not in the room, she resolved to leave the letter where it would meet her eye, and thus prepare the way for a future conversation. When she saw Euphra and Harry, she would have retired immediately; but Euphra, annoyed by her entrance, was now quite able to speak.

"What do you want?" she said angrily.

"This is your letter, Miss Cameron, is it not?" said Margaret, advancing with it in her hand.

Euphra took it, glanced at the direction, pushed Harry away from her, started up in a passion, and let loose the whole gathered irritability of contempt, weariness, disappointment, and suffering, upon Margaret. Her dark eyes flashed with rage, and her sallow cheek glowed like a peach.

"What right have you, pray, to handle my

letters? How did you get this? It has never been posted! And open, too, I declare! I suppose you have read it?"

Margaret was afraid of exciting more wrath before she had an opportunity of explaining; but Euphra gave her no time to think of a reply.

"You *have* read it, you shameless woman! Why don't you lie, like the rest of your tribe, and keep me from dying with indignation? Impudent prying! My maid never posted it, and you have found it and read it! Pray, did you hope to find a secret worth a bribe?"

She advanced on Margaret till within a foot of her.

"Why don't you answer, you hussy? I will go this instant to your mistress. You or I leave the house."

Margaret had stood all this time quietly, waiting for an opportunity to speak. Her face was very pale, but perfectly still, and her eyes did not quail. She had not in the least lost her self-possession. She would not say at once that she had read the letter, because that would instantly rouse the tornado again.

"You do not know my name, Miss Cameron; of course you could not."

"Your name! What is that to me?"

"That," said Margaret, pointing to the letter, "is my father's name."

Euphra looked at her own direction again, and then looked at Margaret. She was so bewildered, that if she had any thoughts, she did not know them. Margaret went on:

"My father is dead. My mother sent the letter to me."

"Then you *have* had the impertinence to read it!"

"It was my duty to read it."

"Duty! What business had you with it?"

Euphra felt ashamed of the letter as soon as she found that she had applied to a man whose daughter was a servant. Margaret answered:

"I could at least reply to it so far, that the writer should not think my father had neglected it. I did not know who it was from till I came to the end."

Euphra turned her back on her, with the words:

"You may go."

Margaret walked out of the room with an unconscious stately gentleness.

"Come back," cried Euphra.

Margaret obeyed.

"Of course you will tell all your fellow-servants the contents of this foolish letter."

Margaret's face flushed, and her eye flashed, at the first words of this speech; but the last words made her forget the first, and to them only she replied. Clasping her hands, she said:

"Dear Miss Cameron, do not call it foolish. For God's sake, do not call it foolish."

"What is it to you? Do you think I am going to make a confidante of *you*?"

Margaret again left the room. Notwithstanding that she had made no answer to her insult, Euphra felt satisfied that her letter was safe from profanation.

No sooner was Margaret out of sight, than, with the reaction common to violent tempers, which in this case resulted the sooner, from the exhaustion produced in a worn frame by the violence of the outburst, Euphra sat down, in a hopeless, unresting way upon the chair from which she had just risen, and began weeping more bitterly than before. She was not only exhausted, but ashamed; and to these feelings was added a far greater sense of disappointment than she could have believed possible, at the frustration of the hope of help from David Elginbrod. True, this hope had been small; but where there is only one hope, its death is equally bitter, whether it be a great or a little hope. And there is often no power of reaction, in a mind which has been gradually reduced to one little faint hope, when that hope goes out in darkness. There is a recoil which is very helpful, from the blow that kills a great hope.

All this time Harry had been looking on, in a kind of paralysed condition, pale with perplexity and distress. He now came up to Euphra, and, trying to pull her hand gently from her face, said:

"What is it all about, Euphra, dear?"

"Oh! I have been very naughty, Harry."

"But what is it all about? May I read the letter?"

"If you like," answered Euphra, listlessly.

Harry read the letter with quivering features. Then, laying it down on the table with a reverential slowness, went to Euphra, put his arms round her and kissed her.

"Dear, dear Euphra, I did not know you were so unhappy. I will find God for you. But first I will—what shall I do to the bad man? Who is it? I will——"

Harry finished the sentence by setting his teeth hard.

"Oh! you can't do anything for me, Harry, dear. Only mind you don't say anything about it to any one. Put the letter in the fire there for me."

"No—that I won't," said Harry, taking up the letter, and holding it tight. "It is a beautiful letter, and it does me good. Don't you think, though it is not sent to God himself, he may read it, and take it for a prayer?"

"I wish he would, Harry."

"But it was very wrong of you, Euphra, dear, to speak as you did to the daughter of such a good man."

"Yes, it was."

"But then, you see, you got angry before you knew who she was."

"But I shouldn't have got angry before I knew all about it."

"Well, you have only to say you are sorry, and Margaret won't think anything more about it. Oh, she is so good!"

Euphra recoiled from making confession of wrong to a lady's-maid; and, perhaps, she was a little jealous of Harry's admiration of Margaret. For Euphra had not yet cast off all her old habits of mind, and one of them was the desire to be first with every one whom she cared for. She had got rid of a worse, which was, a necessity of being first in every company, whether she cared for the persons composing it, or not.

Mental suffering had driven the latter far enough from her; though it would return worse than ever, if her mind were not filled with truth in the place of ambition. So she did not respond to what Harry said. Indeed, she did not speak again, except to beg him to leave her alone. She did not make her appearance again that day.

But at night, when the household was retiring, she rose from the bed on which she had been lying half-unconscious, and going to the door, opened it a little way, that she might hear when Margaret should pass from Mrs. Elton's room towards her own. She waited for some time; but judging, at length, that she must have passed without her knowledge, she went and knocked at her door. Margaret opened it a little, after a moment's delay, half-undressed.

"May I come in, Margaret?"

"Pray, do, Miss Cameron," answered Margaret.

And she opened the door quite. Her cap

was off, and her rich dark hair fell on her shoulders, and streamed thence to her waist. Her under-clothing was white as snow.

"What a lovely skin she has!" thought Euphra, comparing it with her own tawny complexion. She felt, for the first time, that Margaret was beautiful—yes, more: that whatever her gown might be, her form and her *skin* (give me a prettier word, kind reader, for a beautiful fact, and I will gladly use it) were those of one of nature's ladies. She was soon to find that her intellect and spirit were those of one of God's ladies.

"I am very sorry, Margaret, that I spoke to you as I did to-day."

"Never mind it, Miss Cameron. We cannot help being angry sometimes. And you had great provocation under the mistake you made. I was only sorry because I knew it would trouble you afterwards. Please don't think of it again."

"You are very kind, Margaret."

"I regretted my father's death, for the first

time, after reading your letter, for I knew he could have helped you. But it was very foolish of me, for God is not dead."

Margaret smiled as she said this, looking full in Euphra's eyes. It was a smile of meaning unfathomable, and it quite overcame Euphra. She had never liked Margaret before; for, from not very obscure psychological causes, she had never felt comfortable in her presence, especially after she had encountered the nun in the Ghost's Walk, though she had had no suspicion that the nun was Margaret. A great many of our dislikes, both to persons and things, arise from a feeling of discomfort associated with them, perhaps only accidentally present in our minds the first time we met them. But this vanished entirely now.

"Do you, then, know God too, Margaret?"

"Yes," answered Margaret, simply and solemnly.

"Will you tell me about him?"

"I can at least tell you about my father, and what he taught me."

"Oh! thank you, thank you! Do tell me about him—now."

"Not now, dear Miss Cameron. It is late, and you are too unwell to stay up longer. Let me help you to bed to-night. I will be your maid."

As she spoke, Margaret proceeded to put on her dress again, that she might go with Euphra, who had no attendant. She had parted with Jane, and did not care, in her present mood, to have a woman about her, especially a new one.

"No, Margaret. You have enough to do without adding me to your troubles."

"Please, do let me, Miss Cameron. It will be a great pleasure to me. I have hardly anything to call work. You should see how I used to work when I was at home."

Euphra still objected, but Margaret's entreaty prevailed. She followed Euphra to her room. There she served her like a ministering angel; brushed her hair—oh, so gently! smoothing it out as if she loved it. There was health in the touch of her hands, because there was love. She undressed her; covered her in bed as if she had been a child; made up the fire to last as long as possible; bade her good night; and was leaving the room, when Euphra called her. Margaret returned to the bed-side.

"Kiss me, Margaret," she said.

Margaret stooped, kissed her forehead and her lips, and left her.

Euphra cried herself to sleep. They were the first tears she had ever shed that were not painful tears. She slept as she had not slept for months.

In order to understand this change in Euphrasia's behaviour to Margaret—in order, in fact, to represent it to our minds as at all credible—we must remember that she had been trying to do right for some time; that Margaret, as the daughter of David, seemed the only attainable source of the knowledge she sought; that long illness had greatly weakened her obstinacy; that her soul hungered, without knowing it, for love; and that she was naturally gifted with a strong will, the position in which she stood in relation to the count proving only that it was not strong enough, and not that it was weak. Such a character must, for any good, be ruled by itself, and not by circumstances. To have been overcome in the process of time by the persistent goodness of Margaret, might have been the blessed fate of a weaker and worse woman; but if Euphra did not overcome herself, there was no hope of further victory. If Margaret could even wither the power of her oppressor, it would be but to transfer the lordship from a bad man to a good woman; and that would not be enough. It would not be freedom. And indeed, the aid that Margaret had to give her, could only be bestowed on one who already had freedom enough to act in *some* degree from duty. She knew she ought to go and apologize to Margaret. She went.

In Margaret's presence, and in such a mood, she was subjected at once to the holy enchantment of her loving-kindness. She had never received any tenderness from a woman before. Perhaps she had never been in the right mood to profit by it if she had. Nor had she ever before seen what Margaret was. It was only when service—*divine service*—flowed from her in full outgoing, that she reached the height of her loveliness. Then her whole form was beautiful. So was it interpenetrated by, and respondent to, the uprising soul within, that it radiated thought and feeling as if it had been all spirit. This beauty rose to its best in her eyes. When she was ministering to any one in need, her eyes seemed to worship the object of her faithfulness, as if all the time she felt that she was *doing it unto Him*. Her deeds were devotion. She was the receiver and not the giver. Before this, Euphra had seen only the still waiting face; and, as I have said, she had been repelled by it. Once within the sphere of the radiation of her attraction, she was drawn towards her, as towards the haven of her peace: she loved her.

To this, at length, had her struggle with herself in the silence of her own room, and her meditations on her couch, conducted her. Shall we say that these alone had been and were leading her? Or that to all these there was a hidden root, and an informing spirit? Who would not rather believe that his thoughts come from an infinite, self-sphered, self-constituting thought, than that they rise somehow out of a blank abyss of darkness, and are only thought when he thinks them, which thinking he cannot pre-determine or even foresee?

When Euphra woke, her first breath was like a deep draught of spiritual water. She felt as if some sorrow had passed from her, and some gladness come in its stead. She thought and thought, and found that the gladness was Margaret. She had scarcely made the discovery, when the door gently opened, and Margaret peeped in to see if she were awake.

"May I come in?" she said.

"Yes, please, Margaret."

"How do you feel to-day?"

"Oh, so much better, dear Margaret! Your kindness will make me well."

"I am so glad! Do lie still a while, and I will bring you some breakfast. Mrs. Elton will be so pleased to find you let me wait on you!"

"She asked me, Margaret, if you should; but I was too miserable—and too naughty, for I did not like you."

"I knew that; but I felt sure you would not dislike me always."

"Why?"

"Because I could not help loving you."

"Why did you love me?"

"I will tell you half the reason.—Because you looked unhappy."

"What was the other half?"

"That I cannot—I mean I will not tell you."

"Never?"

"Perhaps never. But I don't know.—Not now."

"Then I must not ask you?"

"No—please."

"Very well, I won't."

"Thank you. I will go and get your breakfast."

"What can she mean?" said Euphra to herself.

But she would never have found out.

CHAPTER XIV.

DAVID ELGINBROD.

He being dead yet speaketh.

HEB., xi. 4.

In all 'he' did
Some figure of the golden times was hid.

DR. DONNE.

FROM this time, Margaret waited upon Euphra, as if she had been her own maid. Nor had Mrs Elton any cause of complaint, for Margaret was always at hand when she was wanted. Indeed, her mistress was full of her praises. Euphra said little.

Many and long were the conversations between the two girls, when all but themselves were asleep. Sometimes Harry made one of the company; but they could always send him away when they wished to be alone. And now the teaching for which Euphra had longed, sprang in a fountain at her own door. It had been nigh her long, and she had not known it, for its hour had not come. Now she drank as only the thirsty drink,—as they drink whose very souls are fainting within them for drought.

But how did Margaret embody her lessons?

The second night, she came to Euphra's room, and said:

"Shall I tell you about my father to-night? Are you able?"

Euphra was delighted. It was what she had been hoping for all day.

"Do tell me. I long to hear about him."

So they sat down; and Margaret began to talk about her childhood; the cottage she lived in; the fir-wood all around it; the work she used to do;—her side, in short, of the story which, in the commencement of this book, I have partly related from Hugh's side. Summer and winter, spring-time and harvest, storm and sunshine, all came into the tale. Her mother came into it often; and often too, though not so often, the grand form of her father appeared, remained for a little while, and then passed away. Every time Euphra saw him thus in the mirror of Margaret's memory, she saw him more clearly than before: she felt as if, soon, she should know him quite well. Sometimes she asked a question or two; but generally she allowed Margaret's words to flow unchecked; for she painted her pictures better when the colours did not dry between. They talked on, or rather, Margaret talked and Euphra listened, far into the night. At length, Margaret stopped suddenly, for she became aware that a long time had passed. Looking at the clock on the chimney-piece, she said:

"I have done wrong to keep you up so late. Come—I must get you to bed. You are an invalid, you know, and I am your nurse as well as your maid."

"You will come to-morrow night, then?"

"Yes, I will."

"Then I will go to bed like a good child."

Margaret undressed her, and left her to the healing of sleep.

The next night she spoke again of her father, and what he taught her. Euphra had thought much about him; and at every fresh touch which the story gave to the portrait, she knew him better; till at last, even when circumstances not mentioned before came up, she seemed to have known them from the beginning.

"What was your father like, Margaret?"

Margaret described him very nearly as I have done, from Hugh's account, in the former part of the story. Euphra said:

"Ah! yes. That is almost exactly as I had fancied him. Is it not strange?"

"It is very natural, I think," answered Margaret.

"I seem now to have known him for years."

But what is most worthy of record is, that ever as the picture of David grew on the vision of Euphra, the idea of God was growing unawares upon her inward sight. She was learning more and more about God all the time. The sight of human excellence awoke a faint Ideal of the divine perfection. Faith came of itself, and abode, and grew; for it needs but a vision of the Divine, and faith in God is straightway born in the soul that beholds it. Thus, faith and sight are one. The being of her father in heaven was no more strange and far off from her, when she had seen such a father on earth as Margaret's was. It was not alone David's faith that begot hers, but the man himself was a faith-begetting presence. He was the evidence of God with them.—Thus he, being dead, yet spoke, and the departed man was a present power.

Euphra began to read the story of the Gospel. So did Harry. They found much on which to desire enlightenment; and they always applied to Margaret for the light they needed. It was long before she ventured to say *I think.* She always said:

"My father used to say——" or

"I think my father would have said——"

It was not until Euphra was in great trouble some time after this, and required the immediate consolation of personal testimony, that Margaret spoke as from herself; and then she spoke with positive assurance of faith. She did not then even say *I think*, but, *I am sure; I know; I have seen.*

Many interviews of this sort did not take place between them before Euphra, in her turn, began to confide her history to Margaret.

It was a strangely different one—full of outward event and physical trouble; but, till it approached the last stages, wonderfully barren as to inward production or developement. It was a history of Euphra's circumstances and peculiarities, not of Euphra herself. Till of late, she had scarcely had any history. Margaret's, on the contrary, was a true history; for, with much of the monotonous in circumstance, it described individual growth, and the change of progress. Where there is no change there can be no history; and as all change is either growth or decay, all history must describe progress or retrogression. The former had now begun for Euphra as well; and it was one proof of it that she told Margaret all I have already recorded for my readers, at least as far as it bore against herself. How much more she told her I am unable to say; but after she had told it, Euphra was still more humble towards Margaret, and Margaret more tender, more full of service, if possible, and more devoted to Euphra.

CHAPTER XV.

MARGARET'S SECRET.

> Love is not love
> Which alters when it alteration finds,
> Or bends with the remover to remove.
>
> SHAKSPERE.—*Sonnet* cxvi.

MARGARET could not proceed very far in the story of her life, without making some reference to Hugh Sutherland. But she carefully avoided mentioning his name. Perhaps no one less calm, and free from the operation of excitement, could have been so successful in suppressing it.

"Ah!" said Euphra, one day, "your history is a little like mine there; a tutor comes into them both. Did you not fall dreadfully in love with him?"

"I loved him very much."

"Where is he now?"

"In London, I believe."

"Do you never see him?"

"No."

"Have you never seen him since he left your home—with the curious name?"

"Yes; but not spoken to him."

"Where?"

Margaret was silent. Euphra knew her well enough now not to repeat the question.

"I should have been in love with him, I know."

Margaret only smiled.

Another day, Euphra said:

"What a good boy that Harry is! And so clever too. Ah! Margaret, I have behaved like the devil to that boy. I wanted to have him all to myself, and so kept him a child. Need I confess all my ugliest sins?"

"Not to me, certainly, dear Miss Cameron. Tell God to look into your heart, and take them all out of it."

"I will. I do.—I even enticed Mr. Sutherland away from him to me, when he was the only real friend he had, that I might have them both."

"But you have done your best to make up for it since."

"I have tried a little. I cannot say I have done my best. I have been so peevish and irritable."

"You could not quite help that."

"How kind you are to excuse me so! It makes me so much stronger to try again."

"My father used to say that God was always finding every excuse for us that could be found; every *true* one, you know; not one false one."

"That does comfort one."

After a pause, Euphra resumed:

"Mr. Sutherland did me some good, Margaret."

"I do not wonder at that."

"He made me think less about Count Halkar; and that was something, for he haunted me. I did not know then how very wicked he was. I did love him once. Oh, how I hate him now!"

And she started up and paced the room like a tigress in its cage.

Margaret did not judge this the occasion to read her a lecture on the duty of forgiveness. She had enough to do to keep from hating the man herself, I suspect. But she tried to turn her thoughts into another channel.

"Mr. Sutherland loved you very much, Miss Cameron."

"He loved me once," said poor Euphra, with a sigh.

"I saw he did. That was why I began to love you too."

Margaret had at last unwittingly opened the door of her secret. She had told the other reason for loving Euphra. But, naturally enough, Euphra could not understand what she meant. Perhaps some of my readers, understanding Margaret's words perfectly, and their reference too, may be so far from understanding Margaret herself, as to turn upon me and say:

"Impossible! *You* cannot have understood her or any other woman."

Well!

"What do you mean, Margaret?"

Margaret both blushed and laughed outright.

"I must confess it," said she at once; "it cannot hurt him now: my tutor and yours are the same."

"Impossible!"

"True."

"And you never spoke all the time you were both at Arnstead?"

"Not once. He never knew I was in the house."

"How strange! And you saw he loved me?"

"Yes."

"And you were not jealous?"

"I did not say that. But I soon found that the only way to escape from my jealousy, if the feeling I had was jealousy, was to love you too. I did."

"You beautiful creature! But you could not have loved him much."

"I loved him enough to love you for his sake. But why did he stop loving you? I fear I shall not be able to love him so much now."

"He could not help it, Margaret. I deserved it."

Euphra hid her face in her hands.

"He could not have really loved you, then?"

"Which is better to believe, Margaret," said Euphra, uncovering her face, which two tears were lingering down, and looking up at her—"that he never loved me, or that he stopped loving me?"

"For his sake, the first."

"And for my sake, the second?"

"That depends."

"So it does. He must have found plenty of faults in me. But I was not so bad as he thought me when he stopped loving me."

Margaret's answer was one of her loving smiles, in which her eyes had more share than her lips.

It would have been unendurable to Euphra, a little while before, to find that she had a rival in a servant. Now she scarcely regarded that aspect of her position. But she looked doubtfully at Margaret, and then said:

"How is it that you take it so quietly?—for your love must have been very different from mine. Indeed, I am not sure that I loved him at all; and after I had made up my mind to it quite, it did not hurt me so very much. But you must have loved him dreadfully."

"Perhaps I did. But I had no anxiety about it."

"But that you could not leave to a father such as yours even to settle."

"No. But I could to God. I could trust

God with what I could not speak to my father about. He is my father's father, you know; and so, more to him and me than we could be to each other. The more we love God, the more we love each other; for we find he makes the very love which sometimes we foolishly fear to do injustice to, by loving him most. I love my father ten times more because he loves God, and because God has secrets with him."

"I wish God were a father to me as he is to you, Margaret."

"But he is your father, whether you wish it or not. He cannot be more your father than he is. You may be more his child than you are, but not more than he meant you to be, nor more than he made you for. You are infinitely more his child than you have grown to yet. He made you altogether his child, but you have not given in to it yet."

"Oh! yes; I know what you mean. I feel it is true."

"The Prodigal Son was his father's child.

He knew it, and gave in to it. He did not say: 'I wish my father loved me enough to treat me like a child again.' He did not say that, but—*I will arise and go to my father.*"

Euphra made no answer, but wept. Margaret said no more.

Euphra was the first to resume.

"Mr. Sutherland was very kind, Margaret. He promised—and I know he will keep his promise—to do all he could to help me. I hope he is finding out where that wicked count is."

"Write to him, and ask him to come and see you. He does not know where you are."

"But I don't know where he is."

"I do."

"Do you?" rejoined Euphra with some surprise.

"But he does not know where I am. I will give you his address, if you like."

Euphra pondered a little. She would have liked very much to see him, for she was anxious to know of his success. The love she had felt for him was a very small obstacle to their meeting now; for her thoughts had been occupied with affairs, before the interest of which the poor love she had then been capable of, had melted away and vanished—vanished, that is, in all that was restrictive and engrossing in its character. But now that she knew the relation that had existed between Margaret and him, she shrunk from doing anything that might seem to Margaret to give Euphra an opportunity of regaining his preference. Not that she had herself the smallest hope, even had she had the smallest desire of doing so; but she would not even suggest the idea of being Margaret's rival. At length she answered:

"No, thank you, Margaret. As soon as he has anything to report, he will write to Arnstead, and Mrs. Horton will forward me the letter. No—it is quite unnecessary."

Euphra's health was improving a little, though still she was far from strong.

CHAPTER XVI.

FOREBODINGS.

Faust. If heaven was made for man, 'twas made for me.
Good Angel. Faustus, repent; yet heaven will pity thee.
Bad Angel. Thou art a spirit, God cannot pity thee.
Faust. Be I a devil, yet God may pity me.
Bad Angel. Too late.
Good Angel. Never too late if Faustus will repent.
Bad Angel. If thou repent, devils will tear thee in pieces.

. . . .

Old Man. I see an angel hover o'er thy head,
And with a vial full of precious grace,
Offers to pour the same into thy soul.

MARLOWE.—*Doctor Faustus.*

MR. APPLEDITCH had had some business-misfortunes, not of a heavy nature, but sufficient to cast a gloom over the house in Dervish Town, and especially over the face of his spouse, who had set her heart on a new carpet for her drawing-room, and feared she ought not to procure it now. It is wonderful how conscientious some people are towards their balance at the banker's. How the drawing-room, however, could come to want a new carpet is something mysterious, except there is a peculiar power of decay inherent in things deprived of use. These influences operating, however, she began to think that the two scions of grocery were not drawing nine shillings' worth a week of the sap of divinity. This she hinted to Mr. Appleditch. It was resolved to give Hugh warning.

As it would involve some awkwardness to state reasons, Mrs. Appleditch resolved to quarrel with him, as the easiest way of prefacing his discharge. It was the way she took with her maids-of-all-work; for it was grand in itself, and always left her with a comfortable feeling of injured dignity.

As a preliminary course, she began to treat him with still less politeness than before. Hugh was so careless of her behaviour, that this made no impression upon him. But he came to understand it all afterwards, from putting together the remarks of the children, and the partial communications of Mr. Appleditch to Miss Talbot, which that good lady innocently imparted to her lodger.

At length, one day, she came into the room where Hugh was more busy in teaching than his pupils were in learning, and seated herself by the fire to watch for an opportunity. This was soon found. For the boys, rendered still more inattentive by the presence of their mother, could not be induced to fix the least thought upon the matter in hand; so that Hugh was compelled to go over the same thing again and again, without success. At last he said:

"I am afraid, Mrs. Appleditch, I must ask you to interfere, for I cannot get any attention from the boys to-day."

"And how could it be otherwise, Mr. Sutherland, when you keep wearing them out with going over and over the same thing, till they are sick of it? Why don't you go on?"

"How can I go on when they have not learned the thing they are at? That would be to build the chimneys before the walls."

"It is very easy to be witty, sir; but I beg you will behave more respectfully to me in the presence of my children, innocent lambs!"

Looking round at the moment, Hugh caught in his face what the elder lamb had intended for his back, a grimace hideous enough to have procured him instant promotion in the kingdom of apes. The mother saw it too, and added:

"You see you cannot make them respect you. Really, Mr. Sutherland!"

Hugh was about to reply, to the effect that it was useless, in such circumstances, to attempt teaching them at all, some utterance of which sort was watched for as the occasion for his instant dismission; but at that very moment a carriage and pair pulled sharply up at the door, with more than the usual amount of *quadrupedation*, and mother and sons darted simultaneously to the window.

"My!" cried Johnnie, "what a rum go! Isn't that a jolly carriage, Peetie?"

"Papa's bought a carriage!" shouted Peetie.

"Be quiet, children," said their mother, as she saw a footman get down and approach the door.

"Look at that buffer," said Johnnie. "Do come and see this grand footman, Mr. Sutherland. He's such a gentleman!"

A box on the ear from his mother silenced him. The servant entering with some perturbation a moment after, addressed her mistress, for she dared not address any one else while she was in the room:

"Please 'm, the carriage is astin' after Mr. Sutherland."

"Mr. Sutherland?"

"Yes 'm."

The lady turned to Mr. Sutherland, who, although surprised as well, was not inclined to show his surprise to Mrs. Appleditch.

"I did not know you had carriage-friends, Mr. Sutherland," said she, with a toss of her head.

"Neither did I," answered Hugh. "But I will go and see who it is."

When he reached the street, he found Harry on the pavement, who having got out of the carriage, and not having been asked into the house, was unable to stand still for impatience. As soon as he saw his tutor, he bounded to him, and threw his arms round his neck, standing as they were in the open street. Tears of delight filled his eyes.

"Come, come, come," said Harry; "we all want you."

"Who wants me?"

"Mrs. Elton and Euphra and me. Come, get in."

And he pulled Hugh towards the carriage.

"I cannot go with you now. I have pupils here."

Harry's face fell.

"When will you come?"

"In half an hour."

"Hurrah! I shall be back exactly in half an hour then. Do be ready, please, Mr. Sutherland."

"I will."

Harry jumped into the carriage, telling the coachman to drive where he pleased, and be back at the same place in half an hour. Hugh returned into the house.

As may be supposed, Margaret was the means of this happy meeting. Although she saw plainly enough that Euphra would like to see Hugh, she did not for some time make up her mind to send for him. The circumstances which made her resolve to do so were these.

For some days Euphra seemed to be gradually regaining her health and composure of mind. One evening, after a longer talk than usual, Margaret had left her in bed, and had gone to her own room. She was just preparing to get into bed herself, when a knock at her door startled her, and going to it, she saw Euphra standing there, pale as death, with nothing on but her nightgown, notwithstanding the bitter cold of an early and severe frost. She thought at first she must be walking in her sleep, but the scared intelligence of her open eyes, soon satisfied her that it was not so.

"What is the matter, dear Miss Cameron?" she said, as calmly as she could.

"He is coming. He wants me. If he calls me, I must go."

"No, you shall *not* go," rejoined Margaret, firmly.

"I must, I must," answered Euphra, wringing her hands.

"Do come in," said Margaret, "you must not stand there in the cold."

"Let me get into your bed."

"Better let me go with you to yours. That will be more comfortable for you."

"Oh! yes; please do."

Margaret threw a shawl round Euphra, and went back with her to her room.

"He wants me. He wants me. He will

call me soon," said Euphra, in an agonized whisper, as soon as the door was shut. "What *shall* I do!"

"Come to bed first, and we will talk about it there."

As soon as they were in bed, Margaret put her arm round Euphra, who was trembling with cold and fear, and said:

"Has this man any right to call you?"

"No, no," answered Euphra, vehemently.

"Then *don't* go."

"But I am afraid of him."

"Defy him in God's name."

"But besides the fear, there is something that I can't describe, that always keeps telling me—no, not telling me, pushing me—no, drawing me, as if I could not rest a moment till I go. I cannot describe it. I hate to go, and yet I feel that if I were cold in my grave, I must rise and go if he called me. I wish I could tell you what it is like. It is as if some demon were shaking my soul till I yielded and went. Oh! don't despise me. I can't help it."

"My darling, I don't, I can't despise you. You shall not go to him."

"But I must," answered she, with a despairing faintness more convincing than any vehemence; and then began to weep with a slow, hopeless weeping, like the rain of a November eve.

Margaret got out of bed. Euphra thought she was offended. Starting up, she clasped her hands, and said:

"Oh Margaret! I won't cry. Don't leave me. Don't leave me."

She entreated like a chidden child.

"No, no, I didn't mean to leave you for a moment. Lie down again, dear, and cry as much as you like. I am going to read a little bit out of the New Testament to you."

"I am afraid I can't listen to it."

"Never mind. Don't try. I want to read it."

Margaret got a New Testament, and read part of that chapter of St. John's Gospel which speaks about human labour and the bread of life. She stopped at these words:

"For I came down from heaven, not to do mine own will, but the will of him that sent me."

Euphra's tears had ceased. The sound of Margaret's voice, which, if it lost in sweetness by becoming more Scotch when she read the Gospel, yet gained thereby in pathos, and the power of the blessed words themselves, had soothed the troubled spirit a little, and she lay quiet.

"The count is not a good man, Miss Cameron?"

"You know he is not, Margaret. He is the worst man alive."

"Then it cannot be God's will that you should go to him."

"But one does many things that are not God's will."

"But it is God's will that you should *not* go to him."

Euphra lay silent for a few moments. Suddenly she exclaimed:

"Then I *must* not go to him,"—got out of bed, threw herself on her knees by the bedside, and holding up her clasped hands, said, in low tones that sounded as if forced from her by agony:

"I won't! I won't! O God, I will not. Help me, help me!"

Margaret knelt beside her, and put her arm round her. Euphra spoke no more, but remained kneeling, with her extended arms and clasped hands lying on the bed, and her head laid between them. At length Margaret grew alarmed, and looked at her. But she found that she was in a sweet sleep. She gently disengaged herself, and covering her up soft and warm, left her to sleep out her God-sent sleep undisturbed, while she sat beside, and watched for her waking.

She slept thus for an hour. Then lifting her head, and seeing Margaret, she rose quietly, as if from her prayers, and said with a smile:

"Margaret, I was dreaming that I had a mother."

"So you have, somewhere."

"Yes, so I have, somewhere," she repeated,

and crept into bed like a child, lay down, and was asleep again in a moment.

Margaret watched her for another hour, and then seeing no signs of restlessness, but that on the contrary her sleep was profound, lay down beside her, and soon shared in that repose which to weary women and men is God's best gift.

She rose at her usual hour the next day, and was dressed before Euphra awoke. It was a cold grey December morning, with the hoar-frost lying thick on the roofs of the houses. Euphra opened her eyes while Margaret was busy lighting the fire. Seeing that she was there, she closed them again, and fell once more fast asleep. Before she woke again, Margaret had some tea ready for her; after taking which, she felt able to get up. She rose looking more bright and hopeful than Margaret had seen her before.

But Margaret, who watched her intently through the day, saw a change come over her cheer. Her face grew pale and troubled. Now and then her eyes were fixed on vacancy; and again she would look at Margaret with a woebegone expression of countenance; but presently, as if recollecting herself, would smile and look cheerful for a moment. Margaret saw that the conflict was coming on, if not already begun—that at least its shadow was upon her; and thinking that if she could have a talk with Hugh about what he had been doing, it would comfort her a little, and divert her thoughts from herself, even if no farther or more pleasantly than to the count, she let Harry know Hugh's address, as given in the letter to her father. She was certain that, if Harry succeeded in finding him, nothing more was necessary to insure his being brought to Mrs. Elton's. As we have seen, Harry had traced him to Buccleuch Terrace.

Hugh re-entered the house in the same mind in which he had gone out; namely, that after Mrs. Appleditch's behaviour to him before his pupils, he could not remain their tutor any longer, however great his need might be of the pittance he received for his services.

But although Mrs. Appleditch's first feeling had been jealousy of Hugh's acquaintance with "carriage-people," the toadyism which is so essential an element of such jealousy, had by this time revived; and when Hugh was proceeding to finish the lesson he had begun, intending it to be his last, she said:

"Why didn't you ask your friend into the drawing-room, Mr. Sutherland?"

"Good gracious! The drawing-room!" thought Hugh—but answered: "He will fetch me when the lesson is over."

"I am sure, sir, any friends of yours that like to call upon you here, will be very welcome. It will be more agreeable to you to receive them here, of course; for your accommodation at poor Miss Talbot's is hardly suitable for such visitors."

"I am sorry to say, however," answered Hugh, "that after the way you have spoken to me to-day, in the presence of my pupils, I cannot continue my relation to them any longer."

"Ho! ho!" resnorted the lady, indignation

and scorn mingling with mortification; "our grand visitors have set our backs up. Very well, Mr. Sutherland, you will oblige me by leaving the house at once. Don't trouble yourself, pray, to finish the lesson. I will pay you for it all the same. Anything to get rid of a man who insults me before the very faces of my innocent lambs! And please to remember," she added, as she pulled out her purse, while Hugh was collecting some books he had lent the boys, "that when you were starving, my husband and I took you in and gave you employment out of charity—pure charity, Mr. Sutherland. Here is your money."

"Good morning, Mrs. Appleditch," said Hugh; and walked out with his books under his arm, leaving her with the money in her hand.

He had to knock his feet on the pavement in front of the house, to keep them from freezing, for half-an-hour, before the carriage arrived to take him away. As soon as it came up, he jumped into it, and was carried off in triumph by Harry.

Mrs. Elton received him kindly. Euphra held out her hand with a slight blush, and the quiet familiarity of an old friend. Hugh could almost have fallen in love with her again, from compassion for her pale, worn face, and subdued expression.

Mrs. Elton went out in the carriage almost directly, and Euphra begged Harry to leave them alone, as she had something to talk to Mr. Sutherland about.

"Have you found any trace of Count Halkar, Hugh?" she said, the moment they were by themselves.

"I am very sorry to say I have not. I have done my best."

"I am quite sure of that.—I just wanted to tell you, that, from certain indications which no one could understand so well as myself, I think you will have more chance of finding him now."

"I am delighted to hear it," responded Hugh. "If I only had him!"

Euphra sighed, paused, and then said:

"But I am not sure of it. I think he is in London; but he may be in Bohemia, for anything I *know*. I shall, however, in all probability, know more about him within a few days."

Hugh resolved to go at once to Falconer, and communicate to him what Euphra had told him. But he said nothing to her as to the means by which he had tried to discover the count; for although he felt sure that he had done right in telling Falconer all about it, he was afraid lest Euphra, not knowing what sort of a man he was, might not like it. Euphra, on her part, did not mention Margaret's name; for she had begged her not to do so.

"You will tell me when you know yourself?"

"Perhaps.—I will, if I can. I do wish you could get the ring. I have a painful feeling that it gives him power over me."

"That can only be a nervous fancy, surely," Hugh ventured to say.

"Perhaps it is. I don't know. But, still, without that, there are plenty of reasons for wishing to recover it. He will put it to a bad use, if he can. But for your sake, especially, I wish we could get it."

"Thank you. You were always kind."

"No," she replied, without lifting her eyes; "I brought it all upon you."

"But you could not help it."

"Not at the moment. But all that led to it was my fault."

She paused; then suddenly resumed:

"I will confess.—Do you know what gave rise to the reports of the house being haunted?"

"No."

"It was me wandering about it at night, looking for that very ring, to give to the count. It was shameful. But I did. Those reports prevented me from being found out. But I hope not many ghosts are so miserable as I was.—You remember my speaking to you of Mr. Arnold's jewels?"

"Yes, perfectly."

"I wanted to find out, through you, where the ring was. But I had no intention of involving you."

"I am sure you had not."

"Don't be too sure of anything about me. I don't know what I might have been led to do. But I am very sorry. Do forgive me."

"I cannot allow that I have anything to forgive. But tell me, Euphra, were you the creature in white that I saw in the Ghost's Walk one night? I don't mean the last time."

"Very likely," she answered, bending her head yet lower, with a sigh.

"Then who was the creature in black that met you? And what became of you then?"

"Did you see *her*?" rejoined Euphra, turning paler still. "I fainted at sight of her. I took her for the nun that hangs in that horrid room."

"So did I," said Hugh. "But you could not have lain long; for I went up to the spot where you vanished, and found nothing."

"I suppose I got into the shrubbery before I fell. Or the count dragged me in.—But was that really a ghost? I feel now as if it was a good messenger, whether ghost or not, come to warn me, if I had had the courage to listen. I wish I had taken the warning."

They talked about these and other things, till Mrs. Elton, who had made Hugh promise to stay to lunch, returned. When they were seated at table, the kind-hearted woman said:

"Now, Mr. Sutherland, when will you begin again with Harry?"

"I do not quite understand you," answered Hugh.

"Of course you will come and give him lessons, poor boy. He will be broken-hearted if you don't."

"I wish I could. But I cannot—at least yet; for I know his father was dissatisfied with me. That was one of the reasons that made him send Harry to London."

Harry looked wretchedly disappointed, but said nothing.

"I never heard him say anything of the sort."

"I am sure of it, though. I am very sorry he has mistaken me; but he will know me better some day."

"I will take all the responsibility," persisted Mrs. Elton.

"But unfortunately the responsibility sticks too fast for you to take it. I cannot get rid of my share if I would."

"You are too particular. I am sure Mr. Arnold never could have meant that. This is my house too."

"But Harry is his boy. If you will let me come and see him sometimes, I shall be very thankful, though. I may be useful to him without giving him lessons."

"Thank you," said Harry with delight.

"Well, well! I suppose you are so much in request in London that you won't miss him for a pupil."

"On the contrary, I have not a single engagement. If you could find me one, I should be exceedingly obliged to you."

"Dear! dear! dear!" said Mrs. Elton. "Then you *shall* have Harry."

"Oh! yes; please take me," said Harry, beseechingly.

"No, I cannot. I must not."

Mrs. Elton rang the bell.

"James, tell the coachman I want the carriage in an hour."

Mrs. Elton was as submissive to her coachman as ladies who have carriages generally are, and would not have dreamed of ordering the horses out so soon again for herself; but she forgot everything else when a friend was in need of help, and became perfectly *pachydermatous* to the offended looks or indignant hints of that important functionary.

Within a few minutes after Hugh took his leave, Mrs. Elton was on her way to repeat a visit she had already paid the same morning, and to make several other calls, with the express object of finding pupils for Hugh. But in this she was not so successful as she had expected. In fact, no one whom she could think of, wanted such services at present. She returned home quite down-hearted, and all but convinced that nothing could be done before the approach of the London season.

CHAPTER XVII.

STRIFE.

They'll turn me in your arms, Janet,
 An adder and a snake;
But haud me fast, let me not pass,
 Gin ye would be my maik.

They'll turn me in your arms, Janet,
 An adder and an aske;
They'll turn me in your arms, Janet,
 A bale that burns fast.

They'll shape me in your arms, Janet,
 A dove, but and a swan;
And last, they'll shape me in your arms
 A mother-naked man:
Cast your green mantle over me—
 And sae shall I be wan.

Scotch Ballad: Tamlane.

As soon as Hugh had left the house, Margaret hastened to Euphra. She found her in her own room, a little more cheerful, but still strangely depressed. This appearance increased towards the evening, till her looks became quite haggard, revealing an inward conflict of growing agony. Margaret remained with her.

Just before dinner, the upstairs bell, whose summons Margaret was accustomed to obey, rang, and she went down. Mrs. Elton detained her for a few minutes. The moment she was at liberty, she flew to Euphra's room by the back staircase. But, as she ascended, she was horrified to meet Euphra, in a cloak and thick veil, creeping down the stairs like a thief. Without saying a word, the strong girl lifted her in her arms as if she had been a child, and carried her back to her room. Euphra neither struggled nor spoke. Margaret laid her on her couch, and sat down beside her. She lay without moving, and, although wide awake, gave no other sign of existence than an occasional low moan, that seemed to come from a heart pressed almost to death.

Having lain thus for an hour, she broke the silence.

"Margaret, do you despise me dreadfully?"

"No, not in the least."

"Yet you found me going to do what I knew was wrong."

"You had not made yourself strong by thinking about the will of God. Had you, dear?"

"No. I will tell you how it was. I had been tormented with the inclination to go to him, and had been resisting it till I was worn out, and could hardly bear it more. Suddenly all grew calm within me, and I seemed to hate Count Halkar no longer. I thought with myself how easy it would be to put a stop to this dreadful torment, just by yielding to it—only this once. I thought I should then be stronger to resist the next time; for this was wearing me out so, that I must yield the next time, if I persisted now. But what seemed to justify me, was the thought that so I should find out where he was, and be able to tell Hugh; and then he would get the ring for me, and perhaps that would deliver me. But it was very wrong of me. I forgot all about the will of God. I *will* not go again, Margaret. Do you think I may try again to fight him?"

"That is just what you *must* do. All that God requires of you is, to try again. God's child *must* be free. Do try, dear Miss Cameron."

"I think I could, if you would call me Euphra. You are so strong, and pure, and good, Margaret! I wish I had never had any thoughts but such as you have, you beautiful creature! Oh, how glad I am that you found me! Do watch me always."

"I will call you Euphra. I will be your sister-servant—anything you like, if you will only try again."

"Thank you, with all my troubled heart, dear Margaret! I will indeed try again."

She sprang from the couch in a sudden agony, and grasping Margaret by the arm, looked at her with such a terror-stricken face, that she began to fear she was losing her reason.

"Margaret," she said, as if with the voice

as of one just raised from the dead, speaking with all the charnel damps in her throat, "*could* it be that I am in love with him still?"

Margaret shuddered, but did not lose her self-possession.

"No, no, Euphra, darling. You were haunted with him, and so tired that you were not able to hate him any longer. Then you began to give way to him. That was all. There was no love in that."

Euphra's grasp relaxed.

"Do you think so?"

"Yes."

A pause followed.

"Do you think God cares to have me do his will? Is it anything to him?"

"I am sure of it. Why did he make you else? But it is not for the sake of being obeyed that he cares for it, but for the sake of serving you and making you blessed with his blessedness. He does not think about himself, but about you."

"Oh, dear! oh, dear! I must not go."

"Let me read to you again, Euphra."

"Yes, please do, Margaret."

She read the fortieth chapter of Isaiah, one of her father's favourite chapters, where all the strength and knowledge of God are urged to a height, that they may fall in overwhelming profusion upon the wants and fears and unbelief of his children. How should he that calleth the stars by their names forget his people?

While she read, the cloud melted away from Euphra's face; a sweet sleep followed; and the paroxysm was over for the time.

Was Euphra insane? and were these the first accesses of daily fits of madness, which had been growing and approaching for who could tell how long?

Even if she were mad, or going mad, was not this the right way to treat her? I wonder how often the spiritual cure of faith in the Son of Man, the Great Healer, has been tried on those possessed with our modern demons. Is it *proved* that insanity has its origin in the physical disorder which, it is now said, can be shown to accompany it invariably? Let it be so: it yet appears to me that if the physician would, like the Son of Man himself, descend as it were into the disorganized world in which the consciousness of his patient exists, and receiving as fact all that he reveals to him of its condition—for fact it is, of a very real sort—introduce, by all the means that sympathy can suggest, the one central cure for evil, spiritual and material, namely, the truth of the Son of Man, the vision of the perfect friend and helper, with the revelation of the promised liberty of obedience—if he did this, it seems to me that cures might still be wrought as marvellous as those of the ancient time.

It seems to me, too, that that can be but an imperfect religion, as it would be a poor salvation, from which one corner of darkness may hide us; from whose blessed health and freedom a disordered brain may snatch us; making us hopeless outcasts, till first the physician, the student of physical laws, shall interfere and restore us to a sound mind, or the great God's-angel Death crumble the soul-oppressing brain, with its thousand phantoms of pain and fear and horror, into a film of dust in the hollow of the deserted skull.

Hugh repaired immediately to Falconer's chambers, where he was more likely to find him during the day than in the evening. He was at home. He told him of his interview with Euphra, and her feeling that the count was not far off.

"Do you think there can be anything in it?" asked he, when he had finished his relation.

"I think very likely," answered his friend. "I will be more on the outlook than ever. It may, after all, be through the lady herself that we shall find the villain. If she were to fall into one of her trances, now, I think it almost certain she would go to him. She ought to be carefully watched and followed, if that should take place. Let me know all that you learn about her. Go and see her again to-morrow, that we may be kept informed of her experiences, so far as she thinks proper to tell them."

"I will," said Hugh, and took his leave.

But Margaret, who knew Euphra's condition, both spiritual and physical, better than any other, had far different objects for her, through means of the unholy attraction which the count exercised over her, than the discovery of the stolen ring. She was determined that neither sleeping nor waking should she follow his call, or dance to his piping. She should resist to the last, in the name of God, and so redeem her lost will from the power of this devil, to whom she had foolishly sold it.

The next day, the struggle evidently continued; and it had such an effect on Euphra, that Margaret could not help feeling very anxious about the result as regarded her health, even if she should be victorious in the contest. But not for one moment did Margaret quail; for she felt convinced, come of it what might, that the only hope for Euphra lay in resistance. Death, to her mind, was simply nothing in the balançe with slavery of such a sort.

Once—but evidently in a fit of absence—Euphra rose, went to the door, and opened it. But she instantly dashed it to again, and walking slowly back, resumed her seat on the couch. Margaret came to her from the other side of the bed, where she had been working by the window, for the last quarter of an hour, for the sake of the waning light.

"What is it, dear?" she said.

"Oh, Margaret! are you there? I did not know you were in the room. I found myself at the door before I knew what I was doing."

"But you came back of yourself this time."

"Yes I did. But I still feel inclined to go."

"There is no sin in that, so long as you do not encourage the feeling, or yield to it."

"I hate it."

"You will soon be free from it. Keep on courageously, dear sister. You will be in liberty and joy soon."

"God grant it."

"He will, Euphra. I am sure he will."

"I am sure you know, or you would not say it."

A knock came to the street door. Euphra started, and sat in the attitude of a fearful listener. A message was presently brought her, that Mr. Sutherland was in the drawing-room, and wished to see her.

Euphra rose immediately, and went to him. Margaret, who did not quite feel that she could be trusted yet, removed to a room behind the drawing-room, whence she could see Euphra if she passed to go down stairs.

Hugh asked her if she could tell him anything more about Count Halkar.

"Only," she answered, "that I am still surer of his being near me."

"How do you know it?"

"I need not mind telling you, for I have told you before that he has a kind of supernatural power over me. I know it by his drawing me towards him. It is true I might feel it just the same whether he was in America or in London; but I do not think he would care to do it, if he were so far off. I know him well enough to know that he would not wish for me except for some immediate advantage to himself."

"But what is the use of his doing so, when you don't know where he is to be found."

"I should go straight to him, without knowing where I was going."

Hugh rose in haste.

"Put on your bonnet and cloak, and come with me. I will take care of you. Lead me to him, and the ring shall soon be in your hands again."

Euphra hesitated, half rose, but sat down immediately.

"No, no! Not for worlds," she said. "Do not tempt me. I must not—I dare not—I will not go."

"But I shall be with you. I will take care of you. Don't you think I am able, Euphra?"

"Oh, yes! quite able. But I must not go anywhere at that man's bidding."

"But it won't be at his bidding: it will be at mine."

"Ah! that alters the case rather, does it not? I wonder what Margaret would say."

"Margaret! What Margaret?" said Hugh.

"Oh! my new maid," answered Euphra, recollecting herself. "Not being well at present, she is my nurse."

"We shall take a cab as soon as we get to the corner."

"I don't think the count would be able to guide the horse," said Euphra, with a smile. "I must walk. But I *should* like to go. I will. It would be such a victory to catch him in his own toils."

She rose and ran up stairs. In a few minutes she came down again, cloaked and veiled. But Margaret met her as she descended, and leading her into the back drawing-room, said:

"*Are* you going, Euphra?"

"Yes; but I am going with Mr. Sutherland," answered Euphra, in a defensive tone. "It is to please him, and not to obey the count."

"Are you sure it is all to please Mr. Sutherland? If it were, I don't think you would be able to guide him right. Is it not to get rid of your suffering by yielding to temptation, Euphra? At all events, if you go, even should Mr. Sutherland be successful with him, you will never feel that you have overcome him, or he, that he has lost you. He will still hold you fast. Don't go. I am sure you are deceiving yourself."

Euphra stood for a moment, and pouted like a naughty child. Then suddenly throwing her arms about Margaret's neck, she kissed her, and said:

"I *won't* go, Margaret. Here, take my things up stairs for me."

She threw off her bonnet and cloak, and rejoined Hugh in the drawing-room.

"I can't go," she said. "I must not go. I should be yielding to him, and it would make a slave of me all my life."

"It is our only chance for the ring," said Hugh.

Again Euphra hesitated and wavered; but again she conquered.

"I cannot help it," she said. "I would rather not have the ring than go—if you will forgive me."

"Oh, Euphra!" replied Hugh. "You know it is not for myself."

"I do know it. You won't mind then if I don't go?"

"Certainly not, if you have made up your mind. You must have a good reason for it."

"Indeed I have." And even already she felt that resistance brought its own reward.

Hugh went almost immediately, in order to make his report to Falconer, with whom he had an appointment for the purpose.

"She is quite right," said Falconer. "I do not think, in the relation in which she stands to him, that she could safely do otherwise. But it seems to me very likely that this will turn out well for our plans, too. Let her persist; and in all probability he will not only have to resign her perforce, but will so far make himself subject to her in turn, as to seek her who will not go to him. He will pull upon his own rope till he is drawn to the spot where he has fixed it. What remains for you and me to do, is to keep a close watch on the house and neighbourhood. Most likely we shall find the villain before long."

"Do you really think so?"

"The whole affair is mysterious, and has to do with laws with which we are most imperfectly acquainted; but this seems to me a presumption worth acting upon. Is there no one in the house on whom you could depend for assistance—for information, at least?"

"Yes. There is the same old servant that Mrs. Elton had with her at Arnstead. He is a steady old fellow, and has been very friendly with me."

"Well, what I would advise is, that you should find yourself quarters as near the spot as possible; and, besides keeping as much of a personal guard upon the house as you can, engage the servant you mention to let you know, the moment the count makes his appearance. It will probably be towards night when he calls, for such a man may have reasons as well as instincts to make him love the darkness rather than the light. You had better go at once; and when you have found a place, leave or send the address here to me, and towards night-fall I will join you. But we may have to watch for several days. We must not be too sanguine."

Almost without a word, Hugh went to do as Falconer said. The only place he could find suitable, was a public-house at the corner of a back street, where the men-servants of the neighbourhood used to resort. He succeeded in securing a private room in it, for a week, and immediately sent Falconer word of his locality. He then called a second time at Mrs. Elton's, and asked to see the butler. When he came:

"Irwan," said he, "has Herr von Funkelstein called here to-day?"

"No, sir, he has not."

"You would know him, would you not?"

"Yes, sir; perfectly."

"Well, if he should call to-night, or to-morrow, or any time within the next few days, let me know the moment he is in the house. You will find me at the Golden Staff, round the corner. It is of the utmost importance that I should see him at once. But do not let him know that any one wants to see him. You shall not repent helping me in this affair. I know I can trust you."

Hugh had fixed him with his eyes, before he began to explain his wishes. He had found out that this was the best way of securing attention from inferior natures, and that it was especially necessary with London servants; for their superciliousness is cowed by it, and the superior will brought to bear upon theirs. It is the only way a man without a carriage has to command attention from such. Irwan was not one of this sort. He was a country servant, for one difference. But Hugh made his address as impressive as possible.

"I will with pleasure, sir," answered Irwan, and Hugh felt tolerably sure of him.

Falconer came. They ordered some supper, and sat till eleven o'clock. There being then no chance of a summons, they went out together. Passing the house, they saw light in one upper window only. That light would burn there all night, for it was in Euphra's room. They went on, Hugh accompanying Falconer in one of his midnight walks through London, as he had done repeatedly before. From such companionship and the scenes to which Falconer introduced him, he had gathered this fruit, that he began to believe in God for the sake of the wretched men and women he saw in the world. At first it was his own pain at the sight of such misery that drove him, for consolation, to hope in God; so, at first, it was for his own sake. But as he saw more of them, and grew to love them more, he felt that the only hope for them lay in the love of God; and he hoped in God for them. He saw too that a God not both humanly and absolutely divine, a God less than that God shadowed forth in the Redeemer of men, would not do. But thinking about God thus, and hoping in him for his brothers and sisters, he began to love God. Then, last of all, that he might see in him one to whom he could abandon everything, that he might see him perfect and all in all and as he must be—for the sake of God himself, he believed in him as the Saviour of these his sinful and suffering kin.

As early as was at all excusable, the following morning, he called on Euphra. The butler said that she had not come down yet, but he would send up his name. A message was brought back that Miss Cameron was sorry not to see him, but she had had a bad night, and was quite unable to get up. Irwan replied to his inquiry, that the count had not called. Hugh withdrew to the Golden Staff.

A bad night it had been indeed. As Euphra slept well the first part of it, and had no attack such as she had had upon both the preceding nights, Margaret had hoped the worst was over.

Still she laid herself only within the threshold of sleep, ready to wake at the least motion.

In the middle of the night, she felt Euphra move. She lay still to see what she would do. Euphra slipped out of bed, and partly dressed herself; then went to her wardrobe, and put on a cloak with a large hood, which she drew over her head. Margaret lay with a dreadful aching at her heart. Euphra went towards the door. Margaret called her, but she made no answer. Margaret flew to the door, and reached it before her. Then, to her intense delight, she saw that Euphra's eyes were closed. Just as she laid her hand on the door, Margaret took her gently in her arms.

"Let me go, let me go!" Euphra almost screamed. Then suddenly opening her eyes, she stared at Margaret in a bewildered fashion, like one waking from the dead.

"Euphra! dear Euphra!" said Margaret.

"Oh, Margaret! is it really you?" exclaimed Euphra, flinging her arms about her. "Oh, I *am* glad. Ah! you see what I must have been about. I suppose I knew when I was doing it, but I don't know now. I have forgotten all about it. Oh dear! oh dear! I thought it would come to this."

"Come to bed, dear. You couldn't help it. It was not yourself. There is not more than half of you awake, when you walk in your sleep."

They went to bed. Euphra crept close to Margaret, and cried herself asleep again. The next day she had a bad headache. This with her always followed somnambulation. She did not get up all that day. When Hugh called again in the evening, he heard she was better, but still in bed.

Falconer joined Hugh at the Golden Staff, at night; but they had no better success than before. Falconer went out alone, for Hugh wanted to keep himself fresh. Though very strong, he was younger and less hardened than Falconer, who could stand an incredible amount of labour and lack of sleep. Hugh would have given way under the half.

CHAPTER XVIII.

VICTORY.

O my admired mistress, quench not out
The holy fires within you, though temptations
Shower down upon you : clasp thine armour on ;
Fight well, and thou shalt see, after these wars,
Thy head wear sunbeams, and thy feet touch stars.
MASSINGER.—*The Virgin Martyr.*

BUT Hugh could sleep no more than if he had been out with Falconer. He was as restless as a wild beast in a cage. Something would not let him be at peace. So he rose, dressed, and went out. As soon as he turned the corner, he could see Mrs. Elton's house. It was visible both by intermittent moonlight above, and by flickering gaslight below, for the wind bl(r rather strong. There was snow in the air, he knew. The light they had observed last night, was burning now. A moment served to make these observations; and then Hugh's eyes were arrested by the sight of something else—a man walking up and down the pavement in front of Mrs. Elton's house. He instantly stepped into the shadow of a porch to watch him. The figure might be the count's; it might not; he could not be sure. Every now and then the man looked up to the windows. At length he stopped right under the lighted one, and looked up. Hugh was on the point of gliding out, that he might get as near him as possible before rushing on him, when, at the moment, to his great mortification, a policeman emerged from some mysterious corner, and the figure instantly vanished in another. Hugh did not pursue him; because it would be to set all on a single chance, and that a poor one; for if the count, should it be he, succeeded in escaping, he would not return to a spot which he knew to be watched. Hugh, therefore, withdrew once more und[illegible] a porch, and waited. But, whatever might be the cause, the man made his appearance no more. Hugh contrived to keep watch for two hours, in spite of suspicious policemen. He slept late into the following morning.

Calling at Mrs. Elton's, he learned that the count had not been there; that Miss Cameron had been very ill all night; but that she was rather better since the morning.

That night, as the preceding, Margaret had awaked suddenly. Euphra was not in the bed beside her. She started up in an agony of terror; but it was soon allayed, though not removed. She saw Euphra on her knees at the foot of the bed, an old-fashioned four-post one. She had her arms twined round one of the bed-posts, and her head thrown back, as if some one were pulling her backwards by her hair, which fell over her night-dress to the floor in thick, black masses. Her eyes were closed; her face was death-like, almost livid; and the cold dews of torture were rolling down from brow to chin. Her lips were moving convulsively, with now and then the appearance of an attempt at articulation, as if they were set in motion by an agony of inward prayer. Margaret, unable to move, watched her with anxious sympathy and fearful expectation. How long this lasted she could not tell, but it seemed a long time. At length Margaret rose, and longing to have some share in the struggle, however small, went softly, and stood behind her, shadowing her from a feeble ray of moonlight which, through a wind-rent cloud, had stolen into the room, and lay upon her upturned face. There she lifted up her heart in prayer. In a moment after the tension of Euphra's countenance relaxed a little; composure slowly followed; her head gradually rose, so that Margaret could see her face no longer; then, as gradually, drooped forward. Next her arms untwined themselves from the bed-post, and her hands clasped themselves together. She looked like one praying in the intense silence of absorbing devotion. Margaret stood still as a statue.

In speaking about it afterwards to Hugh, Margaret told him that she distinctly remembered hearing, while she stood, the measured steps of a policeman pass the house on the pavement below.

In a few minutes Euphra bowed her head yet lower, and then rose to her feet. She turned round towards Margaret, as if she knew she was there. To Margaret's astonishment, her eyes were wide open. She smiled a most child-like, peaceful, happy smile, and said:

"It is over, Margaret, all over at last. Thank you, with my whole heart. God *has* helped me."

At that moment, the moon shone out full, and her face appeared in its light like the face of an angel. Margaret looked on her with awe. Fear, distress, and doubt had vanished, and she was already beautiful like the blessed. Margaret got a handkerchief, and wiped the cold damps from her face. Then she helped her into bed, where she fell asleep almost instantly, and slept like a child. Now and then she moaned; but when Margaret looked at her, she saw the smile still upon her countenance.

She woke weak and worn, but happy.

"I shall not trouble you to-day, Margaret, dear," said she. "I shall not get up yet, but you will not need to watch me. A great change has passed upon me. I am free. I have overcome him. He may do as he pleases now. I do not care. I defy him. I got up last night in my sleep, but I remember all about it; and, although I was asleep, and felt powerless like a corpse, I resisted him, even when I thought he was dragging me away by bodily force. And I resisted him, till he left me alone. Thank God!"

It had been a terrible struggle, but she had overcome. Nor was this all: she would no more lead two lives, the waking and the sleeping. Her waking will and conscience had asserted themselves in her sleeping acts; and the memory of the somnambulist lived still in the waking woman. Hence her two lives were blended into one life; and she was no more two, but one. This indicated a mighty growth of individual being.

"I woke without terror," she went on to say. "I always used to wake from such a sleep in an agony of unknown fear. I do not think I shall ever walk in my sleep again."

Is not salvation the uniting of all our nature into one harmonious whole—God first in us, ourselves last, and all in due order between? Something very much analogous to the change in Euphra takes place in a man when he first learns that his beliefs must become acts; that his religious life and his human life are one; that he must *do* the thing that he admires. The Ideal is the only absolute Real; and it *must* become the Real in the individual life as well, however impossible they may count it who never try it, or who do not trust in God to effect it, when they find themselves baffled in the attempt.

In the afternoon, Euphra fell asleep, and when she woke, seemed better. She said to Margaret:

"Can it be that it was all a dream, Margaret? I mean my association with that dreadful man. I feel as if it were only some horrid dream, and that I could never have had anything to do with him. I may have been out of my mind, you know, and have told you things which I believed firmly enough then, but which never really took place. It *could* not have been me, Margaret, could it?"

"Not your real, true, best self, dear."

"I have been a dreadful creature, Margaret. But I feel that all that has melted away from me, and gone behind the sunset, which will for ever stand, in all its glory and loveliness, between me and it, an impassable rampart of defence."

Her words sounded strange and excited, but her eye and her pulse were calm.

"How could he ever have had that hateful power over me?"

"Don't think any more about him, dear, but enjoy the rest God has given you."

"I will, I will."

At that moment, a maid came to the door, with Funkelstein's card for Miss Cameron.

"Very well," said Margaret; "ask him to wait. I will tell Miss Cameron. She may wish to send him a message. You may go."

She told Euphra that the count was in the house. Euphra showed no surprise, no fear, no annoyance.

"Will you see him for me, Margaret, if you don't mind; and tell him from me, that I defy him; that I do not hate him, only because I despise and forget him; that I challenge him to do his worst."

She had forgotten all about the ring. But Margaret had not.

"I will," said she, and left the room.

On her way down, she went into the drawing-room, and rang the bell.

"Send Mr. Irwan to me here, please. It is for Miss Cameron."

The man went, but presently returned, saying that the butler had just stepped out.

"Very well. You will do just as well

When the gentleman leaves who is calling now, you must follow him. Take a cab, if necessary, and follow him everywhere, till you find where he stops for the night. Watch the place, and send me word where you are. But don't let him know. Put on plain clothes, please, as fast as you can."

"Yes, Miss, directly."

The servants all called Margaret, *Miss*.

She lingered yet a little, to give the man time. She was not at all satisfied with her plan, but she could think of nothing better. Happily, it was not necessary. Irwan had run as fast as his old legs would carry him to the Golden Staff. Hugh received the news with delight. His heart seemed to leap into his throat, and he felt just as he did, when, deer-stalking for the first time, he tried to take aim at a great red stag.

"I shall wait for him outside the door. We must have no noise in the house. He is a thief, or worse, Irwan."

"Good gracious! And there's the plate all

laid out for dinner on the sideboard!" exclaimed Irwan, and hurried off faster than he had come.

But Hugh was standing at the door long before Irwan got up to it. Had Margaret known who was watching outside, it would have been a wonderful relief to her.

She entered the dining-room, where the count stood impatient. He advanced quickly, acting on his expectation of Euphra, but seeing his mistake, stopped, and bowed politely. Margaret told him that Miss Cameron was ill, and gave him her message, word for word. The count turned pale with mortification and rage. He bit his lip, made no reply, and walked out into the hall, where Irwan stood with the handle of the door in his hand, impatient to open it. No sooner was he out of the house, than Hugh sprung upon him; but the count, who had been perfectly upon his guard, eluded him, and darted off down the street. Hugh pursued at full speed, mortified at his escape. He had no fear at first of overtaking him, for he had found few men his equals in speed and endurance; but he soon saw, to his dismay, that the count was increasing the distance between them, and feared that, by a sudden turn into some labyrinth, he might escape him altogether. They passed the Golden Staff at full speed, and at the next corner Hugh discovered what gave the count the advantage: it was his agility and recklessness in turning corners. But, like the sorcerer's impunity, they failed him at last; for, at the next turn, he ran full upon Falconer, who staggered back, while the count reeled and fell. Hugh was upon him in a moment. "Help!" roared the count, for a last chance from the sympathies of a gathering crowd.

"I've got him," cried Hugh.

"Let the man alone," growled a burly fellow in the crowd, with his fists clenched in his trowser-pockets.

"Let me have a look at him," said Falconer, stooping over him. "Ah! I don't know him. That's as well for him. Let him up, Sutherland."

The bystanders took Falconer for a detective, and did not seem inclined to interfere, all except the carman before mentioned. He came up, pushing the crowd right and left.

"Let the man alone," said he, in a very offensive tone.

"I assure you," said Falconer, "he's not worth your trouble; for——"

"None o' your cursed jaw!" said the fellow, in a louder and deeper growl, approaching Falconer with a threatening mien.

"Well, I can't help it," said Falconer, as if to himself. "Sutherland, look after the count."

"That I will," said Hugh, confidently.

Falconer turned on the carman, who was just on the point of closing with him, preferring that mode of fighting; and saying only: "Defend yourself," retreated a step. The man was good at his fists too, and, having failed in his first attempt, made the best use of them he could. But he had no chance with Falconer, whose coolness equalled his skill.

Meantime, the Bohemian had been watching his chance; and although the contest certainly did not last longer than one minute, found opportunity, in the middle of it, to wrench himself free from Hugh, trip him up, and dart off. The crowd gave way before him. He vanished so suddenly and completely, that it was evident he must have studied the neighbourhood from the retreat-side of the question. With rat-like instinct, he had consulted the holes and corners in anticipation of the necessity of applying to them. Hugh got up, and, directed, or possibly misdirected by the bystanders, sped away in pursuit; but he could hear or see nothing of the fugitive.

At the end of the minute, the carman lay in the road.

"Look after him, somebody," said Falconer.

"No fear of him, sir; he's used to it;" answered one of the bystanders, with the respect which Falconer's prowess claimed.

Falconer walked after Hugh, who soon returned, looking excessively mortified, and feeling very small indeed.

"Never mind, Sutherland," said he. "The

fellow is up to a trick or two; but we shall catch him yet. If it hadn't been for that big fool there—but he's punished enough."

"But what can we do next? He will not come here again."

"Very likely not. Still he may not give up his attempts upon Miss Cameron. I almost wonder, seeing she is so impressible, that she can give no account of his whereabouts. But I presume *clairvoyance* depends on the presence of other qualifications as well. I should like to mesmerize her myself, and see whether she could not help us then."

"Well, why not, if you have the power?"

"Because I have made up my mind not to superinduce any condition of whose laws I am so very partially informed. Besides, I consider it a condition of disease in which, as by sleeplessness for instance, the senses of the soul, if you will allow the expression, are, for its present state, rendered unnaturally acute. To induce such a condition, I dare not exercise a power which itself I do not understand."

CHAPTER XIX.

MARGARET.

For though that ever virtuous was she,
 She was increased in such excellence,
Of thewes good, yset in high bounté,
 And so discreet and fair of eloquence,
 So benign, and so digne of reverence,
And couthé so the poeple's hert embrace,
That each her loveth that looketh in her face.

CHAUCER.—*The Clerk's Tale.*

HUGH returned to Mrs. Elton's, and, in the dining-room, wrote a note to Euphra, to express his disappointment and shame that, after all, the count had foiled him ; but, at the same time, his determination not to abandon the quest, till there was no room for hope left. He sent this up to her, and waited, thinking that she might be on the sofa, and might send for him. A little weary from the reaction of the excitement he had just gone through, he sat down in the corner farthest from the door. The large room was dimly lighted by one untrimmed lamp.

He sat for some time, thinking that Euphra was writing him a note, or perhaps preparing herself to see him in her room. Involuntarily he looked up, and a sudden pang, as at the vision of the disembodied, shot through his heart. A dim form stood in the middle of the room, gazing earnestly at him. He saw the same face which he had seen for a moment in the library at Arnstead—the glorified face of Margaret Elginbrod, shimmering faintly in the dull light. Instinctively he pressed his hands together, palm to palm, as if he had been about to kneel before Madonna herself. Delight, mingled with hope, and tempered by shame, flushed his face. Ghost or none, she brought no fear with her, only awe.

She stood still.

"Margaret!" he said, with trembling voice.

"Mr. Sutherland!" she responded, sweetly.

"Are you a ghost, Margaret?"

She smiled as if she were all spirit, and, advancing slowly, took his joined hands in both of hers.

"Forgive me, Margaret," sighed he, as if with his last breath, and burst into an agony of tears.

She waited motionless, till his passion should subside, still holding his hands. He felt that her hands were so good.

"He is dead!" said Hugh, at last, with an effort, followed by a fresh outburst of weeping.

"Yes, he is dead," rejoined Margaret, calmly. "You would not weep so if you had seen him die as I did—die with a smile like a summer sunset. Indeed, it was the sunset to me; but the moon has been up for a long time now."

She sighed a gentle, painless sigh, and smiled again like a saint. She spoke nearly as Scotch as ever in tone, though the words and pronunciation were almost pure English.—This lapse into so much of the old form, or rather garment, of speech, constantly recurred, as often as her feelings were moved, and especially when she talked to children.

"Forgive me," said Hugh, once more.

"We are the same as in the old days," answered Margaret; and Hugh was satisfied.

"How do you come to be here?" said Hugh, at last, after a silence.

"I will tell you all about that another time. Now I must give you Miss Cameron's message. She is very sorry she cannot see you, but she is quite unable. Indeed, she is not out of bed. But if you could call to-morrow morning, she hopes to be better and to be able to see you. She says she can never thank you enough."

The lamp burned yet fainter. Margaret went, and proceeded to trim it. The virgins that arose must have looked very lovely, trimming their lamps. It is a deed very fair and womanly—the best for a woman—to make the lamp burn. The light shone up in her face, and the hands removing the globe handled it delicately. He saw that the good hands were very beautiful hands; not small, but admirably shaped, and very pure. As she replaced the globe,—

"That man," she said, "will not trouble her any more."

"I hope not," said Hugh; "but you speak confidently: why?"

"Because she has behaved gloriously. She has fought and conquered him on his own ground; and she is a free, beautiful, and good creature of God for ever."

"You delight me," rejoined Hugh. "Another time, perhaps, you will be able to tell me all about it."

"I hope so. I think she will not mind my telling you."

They bade each other good night; and Hugh went away with a strange feeling, which he had never experienced before. To compare great things with small, it was something like what he had once felt in a dream, in which, digging in his father's garden, he had found a perfect marble statue, young as life, and yet old as the hills. To think of the girl he had first seen in the drawing-room at Turriepuffit, idealizing herself into such a creature as that, so grand, and yet so womanly; so lofty, and yet so lovely; so strong, and yet so graceful!

Would that every woman believed in the ideal of herself, and hoped for it as the will of God, not merely as the goal of her own purest ambition! But even if the lower developement of the hope were all she possessed, it would yet be well; for its inevitable failure would soon develope the higher and triumphant hope.

He thought about her till he fell asleep, and dreamed about her till he woke. Not for a moment, however, did he fancy he was in love with her: the feeling was different from any he had hitherto recognized as embodying that passion. It was the recognition and consequent admiration of a beauty which everyone who beheld it must recognize and admire; but mingled, in his case, with old and precious memories, doubly dear now in the increased earnestness of his nature and aspirations, and with a deep personal interest from the fact that, however little, he had yet contributed a portion of the vital food whereby the gracious creature had become what she was.

In the so-called morning, he went to Mrs. Elton's. Euphra was expecting his visit, and he was shown up into her room, where she was lying on a couch by the fire. She received him with the warmth of gratitude added to that of friendship. Her face was pale and thin, but her eyes were brilliant. She did not appear at first sight to be very ill; but the depth and reality of her sickness grew upon him. Behind her couch stood Margaret, like a guardian angel. Margaret could bear the day, for she belonged to it; and therefore she looked more beautiful still than by the lamp-light. Euphra held out a pale little hand to Hugh, and before she withdrew it, led Hugh's towards

Margaret. Their hands joined. How different to Hugh was the touch of the two hands! Life, strength, persistency in the one: languor, feebleness, and fading in the other.

"I can never thank you enough," said Euphra; "therefore I will not try. It is no bondage to remain your debtor."

"That would be thanks indeed, if I had done anything."

"I have found out another mystery," Euphra resumed, after a pause.

"I am sorry to hear it," answered he. "I fear there will be no mysteries left by and by."

"No fear of that," she rejoined, "so long as the angels come down to men." And she turned towards Margaret as she spoke.

Margaret smiled. In the compliment she felt only the kindness.

Hugh looked at her. She turned away, and found something to do at the other side of the room.

"What mystery, then, have you destroyed?"

"Not destroyed it; for the mystery of courage remains. I was the wicked ghost that night in the Ghost's Walk, you know—the white one: there is the good ghost, the nun, the black one."

"Who? Margaret?"

"Yes, indeed. She has just been confessing it to me. I had my two angels, as one whose fate was undetermined; my evil angel in the count—my good angel in Margaret. Little did I think then that the holy powers were watching me in her. I knew the evil one; I knew nothing of the good. I suppose it is so with a great many people."

Hugh sat silent in astonishment. Margaret, then, had been at Arnstead with Mrs. Elton all the time. It was herself he had seen in the study.

"Did you suspect me, Margaret?" resumed Euphra, turning towards her where she sat at the window.

"Not in the least. I only knew that something was wrong about the house; that some being was terrifying the servants, and poor Harry ; and I resolved to do my best to meet it, especially if it should be anything of a ghostly kind."

"Then you do believe in such appearances?" said Hugh.

"I have never met anything of the sort yet. I don't know."

"And you were not afraid?"

"Not much. I am never really afraid of anything. Why should I be?"

No justification of fear was suggested either by Hugh or by Euphra. They felt the dignity of nature that lifted Margaret above the region of fear.

"Come and see me again soon," said Euphra, as Hugh rose to go.

He promised.

Next day he dined by invitation with Mrs. Elton and Harry. Euphra was unable to see him, but sent a kind message by Margaret as he was taking his leave. He had been fearing that he should not see Margaret ; and when she did appear, he was the more delighted; but the interview was necessarily short.

He called the next day, and saw neither Euphra nor Margaret. She was no better. Mrs. Elton said the physicians could discover no definite disease either of the lungs or of any other organ. Yet life seemed sinking. Margaret thought that the conflict which she had passed through, had exhausted her vitality; that, had she yielded, she might have lived a slave; but that now, perhaps, she must die a free woman.

Her continued illness made Hugh still more anxious to find the ring, for he knew it would please her much. Falconer would have applied to the police, but he feared that the man would vanish from London, upon the least suspicion that he was watched. They held many consultations on the subject.

CHAPTER XX.

A NEW GUIDE.

Das Denken ist nur ein Traum des Fühlens, ein erstorbenes Fühlen, ein blass-graues, schwaches Leben.

Thinking is only a dream of feeling; a dead feeling; a pale-grey, feeble life.

NOVALIS.—*Die Lehrlinge zu Sais.*

For where's no courage, there's no ruth nor mone.

Faerie Queene: vi., 7, 18.

ONE morning, as soon as she waked, Euphra said:

"Have I been still all the night, Margaret?"

"Quite still. Why do you ask?"

"Because I have had such a strange and vivid dream, that I feel as if I must have been to the place. It was a foolish question, though; because, of course, you would not have let me go."

"I hope it did not trouble you much."

"No, not much; for though I was with the count, I did not seem to be there in the body at all, only somehow near him, and seeing him. I can recall the place perfectly."

"Do you think it really was the place he was in at the time?"

"I should not wonder. But now I feel so free, so far beyond him and all his power, that I don't mind where or when I see him. He cannot hurt me now."

"Could you describe the place to Mr. Sutherland? It might help him to find the count."

"That's a good idea. Will you send for him?"

"Yes, certainly. May I tell him for what?"

"By all means."

Margaret wrote to Hugh at once, and sent the note by hand. He was at home when it arrived. He hurriedly answered it, and went to find Falconer. To his delight he was at home—not out of bed, in fact.

"Read that."

"Who is it from?"

"Miss Cameron's maid."

"It does not look like a maid's production."

"It is though. Will you come with me?—You know London ten thousand times better than I do. I don't think we ought to lose a chance."

"Certainly not. I will go with you. But perhaps she will not see me."

"Oh! yes, she will, when I have told her about you."

"It will be rather a trial to see a stranger."

"A man cannot be a stranger with you ten minutes, if he only looks at you;—still less a woman."

Falconer looked pleased, and smiled.

"I am glad you think so. Let us go."

When they arrived, Margaret came to them. Hugh told her that Falconer was his best friend, and one who knew London pernaps better than any other man in it. Margaret looked at him full in the face for a moment. Falconer smiled at the intensity of her still gaze. Margaret returned the smile, and said:

"I will ask Miss Cameron to see you."

"Thank you," was all Falconer's reply; but the tone was more than speech.

After a little while, they were shown up to Euphra's room. She had wanted to sit up, but Margaret would not let her; so she was lying on her couch. When Falconer was presented to her, he took her hand, and held it for a moment. A kind of indescribable beam broke over his face, as if his spirit smiled and the smile shone through without moving one of his features as it passed. The tears stood in his eyes. To understand all this look, one would need to know his history as I do. He laid her hand gently on her bosom, and said: "God bless you!"

Euphra felt that God did bless her in the very words. She had been looking at Falconer all the time. It was only fifteen seconds or so; but the outcome of a life was crowded into Falconer's side of it; and the confidence of

Euphra rose to meet the faithfulness of a man of God.—What words those are!—*A man of God!* Have I not written a revelation? Yes —to him who can read it—yes.

"I know enough of your story, Miss Cameron," he said, "to understand without any preface what you choose to tell me."

Euphra began at once:

"I dreamed last night that I found myself outside the street door. I did not know where I was going; but my feet seemed to know. They carried me, round two or three corners, into a wide, long street, which I think was Oxford-street. They carried me on into London, far beyond any quarter I knew. All I can tell further is, that I turned to the left beside a church, on the steeple of which stood what I took for a wandering ghost just lighted there; —only I ought to tell you, that frequently in my dreams—always in my peculiar dreams —the more material and solid and ordinary things are, the more thin and ghostly they appear to me. Then I went on and on, turning left and right too many times for me to remember, till at last I came to a little, old-fashioned court, with two or three trees in it. I had to go up a few steps to enter it. I was not afraid, because I knew I was dreaming, and that my body was not there. It is a great relief to feel that sometimes; for it is often very much in the way. I opened a door, upon which the moon shone very bright, and walked up two flights of stairs into a back room. And there I found him, doing something at a table by candlelight. He had a sheet of paper before him; but what he was doing with it, I could not see. I tried hard; but it was of no use. The dream suddenly faded, and I awoke, and found Margaret.—Then I knew I was safe," she added, with a loving glance at her maid.

Falconer rose.

"I know the place you mean perfectly," he said. "It is too peculiar to be mistaken. Last night, let me see, how did the moon shine?—Yes. I shall be able to tell the very door, I think, or almost."

"Mr. Falconer," said Hugh, humbly, "forgive me. The feeling was involuntary; and if you have detected in it more than I was aware of, you are at least as likely to be right as I am. But you cannot think more highly of Margaret than I do."

And yet Hugh did not know half the good of her then, that the reader does now.

"Well, we had better part now, and meet again at night."

"What time shall I come to you?"

"Oh! about nine I think will do."

So Hugh went home, and tried to turn his thoughts to his story; but Euphra, Falconer, Funkelstein, and Margaret persisted in sitting to him, the one after the other, instead of the heroes and heroines of his tale. He was compelled to lay it aside, and betake himself to a stroll and a pipe.

As he went down stairs, he met Miss Talbot.

"You're soon tired of home, Mr. Sutherland. You haven't been in above half an hour, and you're out again already."

"Why, you see, Miss Talbot, I want a pipe very much."

"Well, you ain't going to the public house to smoke it, are you?"

"No," answered Hugh, laughing. "But you know, Miss Talbot, you made it part of the agreement that I shouldn't smoke indoors. So I'm going to smoke in the street."

"Now, think of being taken that way!" retorted Miss Talbot, with an injured air. "Why, that was before I knew anything about you. Go up stairs directly, and smoke your pipe; and when the room can't hold any more, you can open the windows. *Your* smoke won't do any harm, Mr. Sutherland. But I'm very sorry you quarrelled with Mrs. Appleditch. She's a hard woman, and over fond of her money and her drawing-room; and for those boys of hers—the Lord have mercy on them, for she has none! But she's a true Christian for all that, and does a power of good among the poor people."

"What does she give them, Miss Talbot?"

"Oh!—she gives them—hm–m—tracts and things. You know," she added, perceiving the weakness of her position, "people's souls should come first. And poor Mrs. Appleditch—you see—some folks is made stickier than others, and their money sticks to them, somehow, that they can't part with it—poor woman!"

To this Hugh had no answer at hand; for though Miss Talbot's logic was more than questionable, her charity was perfectly sound; and Hugh felt that he had not been forbearing enough with the mother of the future pastors. So he went back to his room, lighted his pipe, and smoked till he fell asleep over a small volume of morbid modern divinity, which Miss Talbot had lent him. I do not mention the name of the book, lest some of my acquaintance should abuse me, and others it, more than either deserves. Hugh, however, found the best refuge from the diseased self-consciousness which it endeavoured to rouse, and which is a kind of spiritual somnambulism, in an hour of God's good sleep, into a means of which the book was temporarily elevated. When he woke he found himself greatly refreshed by the influence it had exercised upon him.

It was now the hour for the daily pretence of going to dine. So he went out. But all he had was some bread, which he ate as he walked about. Loitering here, and trifling there, passing five minutes over a volume on every bookstall in Holborn, and comparing the shapes of the meerschaums in every tobacconist's window, time ambled gently along with him; and it struck nine just as he found himself at Falconer's door.

"You are ready, then?" said Falconer.

"Quite."

"Will you take anything before you go? I think we had better have some supper first. It is early for our project."

This was a welcome proposal to Hugh. Cold meat and ale were excellent preparatives for what might be required of him; for a tendency to collapse in a certain region, called by courtesy the chest, is not favourable to deeds of valour. By the time he had spent ten minutes in the discharge of the agreeable duty suggested, he felt himself ready for anything that might fall to his lot.

The friends set out together; and, under the guidance of the two foremost bumps upon Falconer's forehead, soon arrived at the place he judged to be that indicated by Euphra. It was very different from the place Hugh had pictured to himself. Yet in everything it corresponded to her description.

"Are we not great fools, Sutherland, to set out on such a chase, with the dream of a sick girl for our only guide?"

"I am sure you don't think so, else you would not have gone."

"I think we can afford the small risk to our reputation involved in the chase of this same wild-goose. There is enough of strange testimony about things of the sort to justify us in attending to the hint. Besides, if we neglected it, it would be mortifying to find out some day, perhaps a hundred years after this, that it was a true hint. It is altogether different from giving ourselves up to the pursuit of such things.—But this ought to be the house," he added, going up to one that had a rather more *respectable* look than the rest.

He knocked at the door. An elderly woman half opened it, and looked at them suspiciously.

"Will you take my card to the foreign gentleman who is lodging with you, and say I am happy to wait upon him?" said Falconer.

She glanced at him again, and turned inwards, hesitating whether to leave the door half-open or not. Falconer stood so close to it, however, that she was afraid to shut it in his face.

"Now, Sutherland, follow me," whispered Falconer, as soon as the woman had disappeared on the stair.

Hugh followed behind the moving tower of his friend, who strode with long, noiseless strides till he reached the stair. That he took three steps at a time. They went up two flights, and reached the top just as the woman was laying her hand on the lock of the back-room door. She turned and faced them.

"Speak one word," said Falconer, in a hissing whisper, "and ——"

He completed the sentence by an awfully threatening gesture. She drew back in terror, and yielded her place at the door.

"Come in," bawled some one, in second answer to the knock she had already given.

"It *is* he!" said Hugh, trembling with excitement.

"Hush!" said Falconer, and went in.

Hugh followed. He knew the back of the count at once. He was seated at a table, apparently writing; but, going nearer, they saw that he was drawing. A single closer glance showed them the portrait of Euphra growing under his hand. In order to intensify his will and concentrate it upon her, he was drawing her portrait from memory. But at the moment they caught sight of it, the wretch, aware of a hostile presence, sprang to his feet, and reached the chimney-piece at one bound, whence he caught up a sword.

"Take care, Falconer," cried Hugh; "that weapon is poisoned. He is no every-day villain you have to deal with."

He remembered the cat.

Funkelstein made a sudden lunge at Hugh, his face pale with hatred and anger. But a blow from Falconer's huge fist, travelling faster than the point of his weapon, stretched him on the floor. Such was Falconer's impetus, that it hurled both him and the table across the fallen villain. Falconer was up in a moment. Not so Funkelstein. There was plenty of time for Hugh to secure the rapier, and for Falconer to secure its owner, before he came to himself.

"Where's my ring?" said Hugh, the moment he opened his eyes.

"Gentlemen, I protest," began Funkelstein, in a voice upon which the cord that bound his wrists had an evident influence.

"No chaff!" said Falconer. "We've got all our feathers. Hand over the two rings, or be the security for them yourself."

"What witness have you against me?"

"The best of witnesses—Miss Cameron."

"And me," added Hugh.

"Gentlemen, I am very sorry. I yielded to temptation. I meant to restore the diamond after the joke had been played out, but I was forced to part with it."

"The joke is played out, you see," said Falconer. "So you had better produce the other bauble you stole at the same time."

"I have not got it."

"Come, come, that's too much. Nobody would give you more than five shillings for it. And you knew what it was worth when you took it. Sutherland, you stand over him while I search the room. This portrait may as well be put out of the way first."

As he spoke, Falconer tore the portrait and threw it into the fire. He then turned to a cupboard in the room. Whether it was that Funkelstein feared further revelations, I do not know, but he quailed.

"I have not got it," he repeated, however.

"You lie," answered Falconer.

"I would give it you if I could."

"You shall."

The Bohemian looked contemptible enough now, despite the handsomeness of his features. It needed freedom, and the absence of any urgency, to enable him to personate a gentleman. Given those conditions, he succeeded. But as soon as he was disturbed, the gloss vanished and the true nature came out, that of a ruffian and a sneak. He quite quivered at the look with which Falconer turned again to the cupboard.

"Stop," he cried; "here it is."

And muttering what sounded like curses, he pulled out of his bosom the ring, suspended from his neck.

"Sutherland," said Falconer, taking the ring, "secure that rapier, and be careful with it. We will have its point tested. Meantime,"—here he turned again to his prisoner—"I give you warning that the moment I leave this house, I go to Scotland Yard.—Do you know the place? I there recommend the police to look after you, *and they will mind what I say.* If you leave London, a message will be sent, wherever you go, that you had better be watched. My advice to you is, to stay where you are as long as you can. I shall meet you again."

They left him on the floor, to the care of his landlady, whom they found outside the room, speechless with terror.

As soon as they were in the square, on which the moon was now shining, as it had shone in Euphra's dream the night before, Falconer gave the ring to Hugh.

"Take it to a jeweller's, Sutherland, and get it cleaned, before you give it to Miss Cameron."

"I will," answered Hugh, and added, "I don't know how to thank you."

"Then don't," said Falconer, with a smile.

When they reached the end of the street, he turned, and bade Hugh good night.

"Take care of that cowardly thing. It may be as you say."

Hugh turned towards home. Falconer dived into a court, and was out of sight in a moment.

CHAPTER XXI.

THE LAST GROAT.

Thou hast been
As one, in suffering all, that suffers nothing;
A man that fortune's buffets and rewards
Hast ta'en with equal thanks; and blessed are those
Whose blood and judgment are so well commingled
That they are not a pipe for Fortune's finger
To sound what stop she please.

Hamlet.

Most friends befriend themselves with friendship's show.

SOUTHWELL.

HUGH took the ring to Mrs. Elton's, and gave it into Margaret's hand. She brought him back a message of warmest thanks from Euphra. She had asked for writing materials at once, and was now communicating the good news to Mr. Arnold, in Madeira.

"I have never seen her look so happy," added Margaret. "She hopes to be able to see you in the evening, if you would not mind calling again."

Hugh did call, and saw her. She received him most kindly. He was distressed to see how altered she was. The fire of one life seemed dying out—flowing away and spending from her eyes, which it illuminated with too much light as it passed out. But the fire of another life, the immortal life, which lies in thought and feeling, in truth and love divine, which death cannot touch, because it is not of his kind, was growing as fast. He sat with her for an hour, and then went.

This chapter of his own history concluded, Hugh returned with fresh energy to his novel, and worked at it as his invention gave him scope. There was the more necessity that he should make progress, from the fact that, having sent his mother the greater part of the salary he had received from Mr. Arnold, he was now reduced to his last sovereign.

Poverty looks rather ugly when she comes so close as this. But she had not yet accosted him; and with a sovereign in his pocket, and last week's rent paid, a bachelor is certainly not poverty-stricken, at least when he is as independent, not only of other people, but of himself, as Hugh was. Still, without more money than that a man walks in fetters, and is ready to forget that the various restraints he is under are not incompatible with most honourable freedom. So Hugh worked as hard as he could to finish his novel, and succeeded within a week. Then the real anxiety began. He carried it, with much doubtful hope, to one of the principal publishing houses. Had he been more selfishly wise, he would have put it into the hands of Falconer to negotiate for him. But he thought he had given him quite trouble enough already. So he went without an introduction even. The manuscript was received politely, and attention was promised. But a week passed, and another, and another. A human soul was in commotion about the meat that perisheth—and the manuscript lay all the time unread,—forgotten in a drawer.

At length he reached his last coin. He had had no meat for several days, except once that he dined at Mrs. Elton's. But he would not borrow till absolutely compelled, and sixpence would keep him alive another day. In the morning he had some breakfast (for he knew his books were worth enough to pay all he owed Miss Talbot), and then he wandered out. Through the streets he paced and paced, looking in at all the silversmiths' and printsellers' windows, and solacing his poverty with a favourite amusement of his in uneasy circumstances, an amusement cheap enough for a Scotchman reduced to his last sixpence—castle-building. This is not altogether a bad employment where hope has laid the foundation; but it is rather a heartless one where the imagination has to draw the ground plan as well as the elevations. The latter, however, was not quite Hugh's condition yet.—He returned at night, carefully avoiding the cook-shops and their kindred snares, with a silver groat in his pocket still. But he crawled up stairs rather feebly, it must be confessed, for a youth with limbs moulded in the fashion of his.

He found a letter waiting him, from a friend of his mother, informing him that she was dangerously ill, and urging him to set off immediately for home. This was like the blast of fiery breath from the dragon's maw, which overthrew the Red-cross knight—but into the well of life, where all his wounds were healed, and—and—well—board and lodging provided him gratis.

When he had read the letter, he fell on his knees, and said to his father in heaven: "What am I to do?"

There was no lake with golden pieces in its bottom, whence a fish might bring him a coin. Nor in all the wide London lay there one he could claim as his, but the groat in his pocket.

He rose with the simple resolution to go and tell Falconer. He went. He was not at home. Emboldened by necessity, Hugh left his card, with the words on it: "Come to me; I need you." He then returned, packed a few necessaries, and sat down to wait. But he had not sat five minutes before Falconer entered.

"What's the matter, Sutherland, my dear fellow? You haven't pricked yourself with that skewer, have you?"

Hugh handed him the letter with one hand; and when he had read it, held out the four-penny piece in the other hand, to be read likewise. Falconer understood at once.

"Sutherland," he said, in a tone of reproof, "it is a shame of you to forget that men are brothers. Are not two who come out of the heart of God, as closely related as if they had lain in the womb of one mother? Why did you not tell me? You have suffered—I am sure you have."

"I have—a little," Hugh confessed. "I am getting rather low in fact. I haven't had quite enough to eat."

He said this to excuse the tears which

Falconer's kindness—not hunger—compelled from their cells.

"But," he added, "I would have come to you as soon as the fourpence was gone; or at least, if I hadn't got another before I was very hungry again."

"Good heavens!" exclaimed Falconer, half angrily. Then pulling out his watch, "We have two hours," said he, "before a train starts for the north. Come to my place."

Hugh rose and obeyed. Falconer's attendant soon brought them a plentiful supper from a neighbouring shop; after which Falconer got out one of his bottles of port, well known to his more intimate friends; and Hugh thought no more about money than if he had had his purse full. If it had not been for anxiety about his mother, he would have been happier than he had ever been in his life before. For, crossing in the night the wavering, heaving morass of the world, had he not set his foot upon one spot which did not shake; the summit, indeed, of a mighty Plutonic rock, that went down widening away to the very centre of the earth? As he sped along in the railway that night, the prophecy of thousands of years came back: "A man shall be a hiding place from the wind, a covert from the tempest, the shadow of a great rock in a weary land." And he thought it would be a blessed time indeed, when this was just what a man was. And then he thought of the Son of Man, who, by being such first, was enabling all his friends to be such too. Of him Falconer had already learned this 'truth in the inward parts'; and had found, in the process of learning it, that this was the true nature which God had made his from the first, no new thing superinduced upon it. He had had but to clear away the rubbish of worldliness, which more or less buries the best natures for a time, and so to find himself.

After Hugh had eaten and drunk, and thus once more experienced the divinity that lay in food and wine, he went to take leave of his friends at Mrs. Elton's. Like most invalids, Euphra was better in the evening: she requested to see him. He found her in bed, and much wasted since he saw her last. He could not keep the tears from filling his eyes, for all the events of that day had brought them near the surface.

"Do not cry, dear friend," she said sweetly. "There is no room for me here any more, and I am sent for."

Hugh could not reply. She went on:

"I have written to Mr. Arnold about the ring, and all you did to get it. Do you know he is going to marry Lady Emily?"

Still Hugh could not answer.

Margaret stood on the other side of the bed, the graceful embodiment of holy health, and, in his sorrow, he could not help feeling the beauty of her presence. Her lovely hands were the servants of Euphra, and her light, firm feet moved only in ministration. He felt that Euphra had room in the world while Margaret waited on her. It is not house, and fire, and plenty of servants, and all the things that money can procure, that make a home

—not father or mother or friends; but one heart which will not be weary of helping, will not be offended with the petulance of sickness, nor the ministrations needful to weakness: this "entire affection hating nicer hands" will make a home of a cave in a rock, or a gipsy's tent. This Euphra had in Margaret, and Hugh saw it.

"I trust you will find your mother better, Hugh," said Euphra.

"I fear not," answered he.

"Well, Margaret has been teaching me, and I think I have learned it, that death is not at all such a dreadful thing as it looks. I said to her: 'It is easy for you, Margaret, who are so far from death's door.' But she told me that she had been all but dead once, and that you had saved her life almost with your own. Oh, Hugh! she is such a dear!"

Euphra smiled with ten times the fascination of any of her old smiles; for the soul of the smile was love.

"I shall never see you again, I daresay,"

she went on. "My heart thanks you, from its very depths, for your goodness to me. It has been a thousand times more than I deserve."

Hugh kissed in silence the wasted hand held out to him in adieu, and departed. And the world itself was a sad wandering star.

Falconer had called for him. They drove to Miss Talbot's, where Hugh got his 'bag of needments,' and bade his landlady good-bye for a time. Falconer then accompanied him to the railway.

Having left him for a moment, Falconer rejoined him, saying: "I have your ticket;" and put him into a first-class carriage.

Hugh remonstrated. Falconer replied:

"I find this hulk of mine worth taking care of. You will be twice the good to your mother, if you reach her tolerably fresh."

He stood by the carriage door talking to him, till the train started; walked alongside till it was fairly in motion; then, bidding him good-bye, left in his hand a little packet, which Hugh, opening it by the light of the lamp,

over many cities. She to whose memory this book is dedicated, is—I will not say *was*—one of the noblest of such.

There are two ways of accounting for the difficulty which a reader may find in believing in such a character: either that, not being poor, he has never needed such a friend; or that, being rich, he has never been such a friend.

Or if it be that, being poor, he has never found such a friend; his difficulty is easy to remove:—*I have.*

CHAPTER XXII.

DEATH.

Think then, my soul, that Death is but a groom
Which brings a Taper to the outward room,
Whence thou spy'st first a little glimmering light;
And after brings it nearer to thy sight:
For such approaches doth heaven make in death.

DR. DONNE.

HUGH found his mother even worse than he had expected; but she rallied a little after his arrival.

In the evening, he wandered out in the bright moonlit snow. How strange it was to see all the old forms with his heart so full of new things! The same hills rose about him, with all the lines of their shapes unchanged in seeming. Yet they were changing as surely as himself; nay, he continued more the same than they; for in him the old forms were folded up in the new. In the eyes of Him who creates time, there is no rest, but a living sacred change, a journeying towards rest. He alone rests; and he alone, in virtue of his rest, creates change.

He thought with sadness, how all the haunts of his childhood would pass to others, who would feel no love or reverence for them; that the house would be the same, but sounding with new steps, and ringing with new laughter. A little further thought, however, soon satisfied him that places die as well as their dwellers; that, by slow degrees, their forms are wiped out; that the new tastes obliterate the old fashions; and that ere long the very shape of the house and farm would be lapped, as it were, about the tomb of him who had been the soul of the shape, and would vanish from the face of the earth.

All the old things at home looked sad. The look came from this, that, though he could sympathize with them and their story, they could not sympathize with him, and he suffused them with his own sadness. He could find no refuge in the past; he must go on into the future.

His mother lingered for some time without any evident change. He sat by her bedside the most of the day. All she wanted was to have him within reach of her feeble voice, that she might, when she pleased, draw him within touch of her feeble hand. Once she said:

"My boy, I am going to your father."

"Yes, mother, I think you are," Hugh replied. "How glad he will be to see you!"

"But I shall leave you alone."

"Mother, I love God."

The mother looked at him, as only a mother can look, smiled sweetly, closed her eyes as with the weight of her contentment, fell asleep holding his hand, and slept for hours.

Meanwhile, in London, Margaret was watching Euphra. She was dying, and

Margaret was the angel of life watching over her.

"I shall get rid of my lameness there, Margaret, shall I not?" said Euphra, one day, half playfully.

"Yes, dear."

"It will be delightful to walk again without pain."

"Perhaps you will not get rid of it all at once, though."

"Why do you think so?" asked Euphra, with some appearance of uneasiness.

"Because, if it is taken from you before you are quite willing to have it as long as God pleases, by and by you will not be able to rest, till you have asked for it back again, that you may bear it for his sake."

"I am willing, Margaret, I am willing. Only one can't like it, you know."

"I know that," answered Margaret.

She spoke no more, and Margaret heard her weeping gently. Half an hour had passed away, when she looked up, and said:

"Margaret, dear, I begin to like my lameness, I think."

"Why, dear?"

"Why, just because God made it, and bade me bear it. May I not think it is a mark on me from his hand?"

"Yes, I think so."

"Why do you think it came on me?"

"To walk back to Him with, dear."

"Yes, yes; I see it all."

Until now, Margaret had not known to what a degree the lameness of Euphra had troubled her. That her pretty ancle should be deformed, and her light foot able only to limp, had been a source of real distress to her, even in the midst of far deeper.

The days passed on, and every day she grew weaker. She did not suffer much, but nothing seemed to do her good. Mrs. Elton was kindness itself. Harry was in dreadful distress. He haunted her room, creeping in whenever he had a chance, and sitting in corners out of the way. Euphra liked to have him near her.

She seldom spoke to him, or to any one but Margaret, for Margaret alone could hear with ease what she said. But now and then she would motion him to her bedside, and say—it was always the same—

"Harry, dear, be good."

"I will; indeed I will, dear Euphra," was still Harry's reply.

Once, expressing to Margaret her regret that she should be such a trouble to her, she said:

"You have to do so much for me, that I am ashamed."

"Do let me wash the feet of one of his disciples;" Margaret replied, gently expostulating; after which, Euphra never grumbled at her own demands upon her.

Again, one day, she said:

"I am not right at all to-day, Margaret. God can't love me, I am so hateful."

"Don't measure God's mind by your own, Euphra. It would be a poor love that depended not on itself, but on the feelings of the person loved. A crying baby turns away from its mother's breast, but she does not put it away till it stops crying. She holds it closer. For my part, in the worst mood I am ever in, when I don't feel I love God at all, I just look up to his love. I say to him: 'Look at me. See what state I am in. Help me!' Ah! you would wonder how that makes peace. And the love comes of itself; sometimes so strong, it nearly breaks my heart."

"But there is a text I don't like."

"Take another, then."

"But it will keep coming."

"Give it back to God, and never mind it."

"But would that be right?"

"One day, when I was a little girl, so high, I couldn't eat my porridge, and sat looking at it. 'Eat your porridge,' said my mother. 'I don't want it,' I answered. 'There's nothings else for you,' said my mother—for she had not learned so much from my father then, as she did before he died. 'Hoots!' said my father—I cannot, dear Euphra, make *his* words into English."

"No, no, don't," said Euphra; "I shall understand them perfectly."

"'Hoots! Janet, my woman!' said my father. 'Gie the bairn a dish o' tay. Wadna ye like some tay, Maggy, my doo?' 'Ay wad I,' said I. 'The parritch is guid eneuch,' said my mother. 'Nae doot aboot the parritch, woman; it's the bairn's stamack, it's no the parritch.' My mother said no more, but made me a cup of such nice tea; for whenever she gave in, she gave in quite. I drank it; and, half from anxiety to please my mother, half from reviving hunger, attacked the porridge next, and ate it up. 'Leuk at that!' said my father. 'Janet, my woman, gie a body the guid that they can tak', an' they'll sune tak' the guid that they canna. Ye're better noo, Maggy, my doo?' I never told him that I had taken the porridge too soon after all, and had to creep into the wood, and be sick. But it is all the same for the story."

Euphra laughed a feeble but delighted laugh, and applied the story for herself.

So the winter days passed on.

"I wish I could live till the spring," said Euphra. "I should like to see a snowdrop and a primrose again."

"Perhaps you will, dear; but you are going into a better spring. I could almost envy you, Euphra."

"But shall we have spring there?"

"I think so."

"And spring-flowers?"

"I think we shall—better than here."

"But they will not mean so much."

"Then they won't be so good. But I should think they would mean ever so much more, and be ever so much more spring-like. They will be the spring-flowers to all winters in one, I think."

Folded in the love of this woman, anointed for her death by her wisdom, baptized for the new life by her sympathy and its tears, Euphra died in the arms of Margaret.

Margaret wept, fell on her knees, and gave God thanks. Mrs. Elton was so distressed, that, as soon as the funeral was over, she broke up her London household, sending some of the servants home to the country, and taking some to her favourite watering place, to which Harry also accompanied her.

She hoped that, now the affair of the ring was cleared up, she might, as soon as Hugh returned, succeed in persuading him to follow them to Devonshire, and resume his tutorship. This would satisfy her anxiety about Hugh and Harry both.

Hugh's mother died too, and was buried. When he returned from the grave which now held both father and mother, he found a short note from Margaret, telling him that Euphra was gone. Sorrow is easier to bear when it comes upon sorrow; but he could not help feeling a keen additional pang, when he learned that she was dead whom he had loved once, and now loved better. Margaret's note informed him likewise that Euphra had left a written request, that her diamond ring should be given to him to wear for her sake.

He prepared to leave the home whence all the

homeness had now vanished, except what indeed lingered in the presence of an old nurse, who had remained faithful to his mother to the last. The body itself is of little value after the spirit, the love, is out of it: so the house and all the old things are little enough, after the loved ones are gone who kept it alive and made it home.

All that Hugh could do for this old nurse was to furnish a cottage for her out of his mother's furniture, giving her everything she liked best. Then he gathered the little household treasures, the few books, the few portraits and ornaments, his father's sword, and his mother's wedding-ring; destroyed with sacred fire all written papers; sold the remainder of the furniture, which he would gladly have burnt too, and so proceeded to take his last departure from the home of his childhood.

CHAPTER XXIII.

NATURE AND HER LADY.

Die Frauen sind ein liebliches Geheimniss, nur verhüllt, nicht verschlossen.—NOVALIS.—*Moralische Ansichten.*

Women are a lovely mystery—veiled, however, not shut up.

Her twilights were more clear than our mid-day;
She dreamt devoutlier than most use to pray.
DR. DONNE.

PERHAPS the greatest benefit that resulted to Hugh from being thus made a pilgrim and a stranger in the earth, was, that Nature herself saw him, and took him in. Hitherto, as I have already said, Hugh's acquaintance with Nature had been chiefly a second-hand one—he knew friends of hers. Nature in poetry—not in the form of Thomsonian or Cowperian descriptions, good as they are, but closely interwoven with and expository of human thought and feeling, had long been dear to him. In this form he had believed that he knew her so well, as to be able to reproduce the lineaments of her beloved face. But now she herself appeared to him—the grand, pure, tender mother, ancient in years, yet ever young; appeared to him, not in the mirror of a man's words, but bending over him from the fathomless bosom of the sky, from the outspread arms of the forest-trees, from the silent judgment of the everlasting hills. She spoke to him from the depths of air, from the winds that harp upon the boughs, and trumpet upon the great caverns, and from the streams that sing as they go to be lost in rest. She would have shone upon him out of the eyes of her infants, the flowers, but they had their faces turned to her breast now, hiding from the pale blue eyes and the freezing breath of old Winter, who was looking for them with his face bent close to their refuge. And he felt that she had a power to heal and to instruct; yea, that she was a power of life, and could speak to the heart and conscience mighty words about God and Truth and Love.

For he did not forsake his dead home in haste. He lingered over it, and roamed about its neighbourhood. Regarding all about him with quiet, almost passive spirit, he was astonished to find how his eyes opened to see nature in the mass. Before, he had beheld only portions and beauties. When or how the change passed upon him he could not tell. But he no longer looked for a pretty eyebrow or a lovely lip on the face of nature: the soul of nature looked out upon him from the harmony of all, guiding him unsought to the discovery of a thousand separate delights; while from the expanded vision new meanings flashed upon him every day. He beheld in the great All the expression of the thoughts and feelings of the maker of the heavens and the earth and the sea and the fountains of water. The powers of the world to come, that is, the world of unseen truth and ideal reality, were upon him in the presence of the world that now is. For the first time in his life, he felt at home with nature; and while he could moan with the wintery wind, he no longer sighed in the wintery sunshine, that foretold, like the far-off flutter of a herald's banner, the approach of victorious lady-spring.

With the sorrow and loneliness of loss within him, and Nature around him seeming to sigh for a fuller expression of the thought that throbbed within her, it is no wonder that the form of Margaret, the gathering of the thousand forms of nature into one intensity and harmony of loveliness, should rise again upon the world of his imagination, to set no more. Father and mother were gone. Margaret remained behind. Nature lay around him like a shining disk, that needed a visible centre of intensest light—a shield of silver, that needed but a diamond boss: Margaret alone could be that centre—that diamond light-giver; for she alone, of all the women he knew, seemed so to drink of the sun-rays of

God, as to radiate them forth, for very fullness, upon the clouded world.

She had dawned on him like a sweet crescent moon, hanging far-off in a cold and low horizon: now, lifting his eyes, he saw that same moon nearly at the full, and high overhead, yet leaning down towards him through the deep blue air, that overflowed with her calm triumph of light. He knew that he loved her now. He knew that every place he went through, caught a glimmer of romance the moment he thought of her; that every most trifling event that happened to himself, looked like a piece of a story-book the moment he thought of telling it to her. But the growth of these feelings had been gradual—so slow and gradual, that when he recognized them, it seemed to him as if he had felt them from the first. The fact was, that as soon as he began to be capable of loving Margaret, he had begun to love her. He had never been able to understand her till he was driven into the desert. But now that Nature revealed herself to him full of Life, yea, of the Life of Life, namely, of God himself, it was natural that he should honour and love that 'lady of her own'; that he should recognize Margaret as greater than himself, as nearer to the heart of Nature—yea, of God the father of all. She had been one with Nature from childhood, and when he began to be one with Nature too, he must become one with her.

And now, in absence, he began to study the character of her whom, in presence, he had thought he knew perfectly. He soon found that it was a Manoa, a golden city in a land of Paradise—too good to be believed in, except by him who was blessed with the beholding of it. He knew now that she had always understood what he was only just waking to recognize. And he felt that the scholar had been very patient with the stupidity of the master, and had drawn from his lessons a nourishment of which he had known nothing himself.

But dared he think of marrying her, a

creature inspired with a presence of the Spirit of God which none but the saints enjoy, and thence clothed with a garment of beauty, which her spirit wove out of its own loveliness? She was a being to glorify any man merely by granting him her habitual presence: what, then, if she gave her love! She would bring with her the presence of God himself, for she walked ever in his light, and that light clung to her and radiated from her. True, many young maidens must be walking in the sunshine of God, else whence the light and loveliness and bloom, the smile and the laugh of their youth? But Margaret not only walked in this light: she knew it and whence it came. She looked up to its source, and it illuminated her face.

The silent girl of old days, whose countenance wore the stillness of an unsunned pool, as she listened with reverence to his lessons, had blossomed into the calm, stately woman, before whose presence he felt rebuked he knew not why, upon whose face lay slumbering thought, ever ready to wake into life and motion. Dared he love her? Dared he tell her that he loved her? Dared he, so poor, so worthless, seek for himself such a world's treasure?—He might have known that worth does not need honour; that its lowliness is content with ascribing it.

Some of my readers may be inclined to think that I hide, for the sake of my hero—poor little hero, one of God's children, learning to walk—an inevitable struggle between his love and his pride; inasmuch as, being but a tutor, he might be expected to think the more of his good family, and the possibility of his one day coming to honour without the drawback of having done anything to merit it, a title being almost within his grasp; while Margaret was a ploughman's daughter, and a lady's maid. But, although I know more of Hugh's faults than I have thought it at all necessary to bring out in my story, I protest that, had he been capable of giving the name of love to a feeling in whose presence pride dared to speak, I should have considered him unworthy of my poor pen. In plain language, I doubt if I should have cared to write his story at all.

He gathered together, as I have said, the few memorials of the old ship gone down in the quiet ocean of Time; paid one visit of sorrowful gladness to his parents' grave, over which he raised no futile stone—leaving it, like the forms within it, in the hands of holy decay; and took his road—whither? To Margaret's home—to see old Janet; and to go once to the grave of his second father. Then he would return to the toil and hunger and hope of London.

What made Hugh go to Turriepuffit? His love to Margaret? No. A better motive even than that:—*Repentance*. Better I mean for Hugh as to the individual occasion; not in itself; for love is deeper than repentance, seeing that without love there can be no repentance. He had repented before; but now that he haunted in silence the regions of the past, the whole of his history in connection with David returned on him clear and vivid, as if passing once again before his eyes and through his heart; and he repented more deeply still. Perhaps he was not quite so much to blame as he thought himself. Perhaps only now was it possible for the seeds of truth, which David had sown in his heart, to show themselves above the soil of lower, yet ministering cares. They had needed to lie a winter long in the earth. Now the keen blasts and griding frosts had done their work, and they began to grow in the tearful prime. Sorrow for loss brought in her train sorrow for wrong—a sister more solemn still, and with a deeper blessing in the voice of her loving farewell.—It is a great mistake to suppose that sorrow is a part of repentance. It is far too good a grace to come so easily. A man may *repent*, that is, *think better of it, and change his way*, and be very much of a Pharisee—I do not say a hypocrite—for a long time after: it needs a saint to be sorrowful. Yet repentance is generally the road to this sorrow.—And now that in the gracious time of grief, his eyesight purified by tears, he entered one after another all the chambers of the past, he humbly renewed once more his friendship with the noble dead, and with the homely, heartful living. The grey-headed man who walked with God like a child, and with his fellow-men like an elder brother who was always forgetting his birthright and serving the younger; the woman who believed where she could not see, and loved where she could not understand; and the maiden who was still and lustreless, because she ever absorbed and seldom reflected the light—all came to him, as if to comfort him once more in his loneliness, when his heart had room for them, and need of them yet again. David now became, after his departure, yet more of a father to him than before. For that spirit, which is the true soul of all this body of things, had begun to recall to his mind the words of David, and so teach him the things that David knew, the everlasting realities of God. And it seemed to him the while, that he heard David himself uttering, in his homely, kingly voice, whatever truth returned to him from the echo-cave of the past. Even when a quite new thought arose within him, it came to him in the voice of David, or at least with the solemn music of his tones clinging about it as the murmur about the river's course. Experience had now brought him up to the point where he could begin to profit by David's communion; he needed the things which David could teach him; and David began forthwith to give them to him.

That birth of nature in his soul, which enabled him to understand and love Margaret, helped him likewise to contemplate with admiration and awe, the towering peaks of David's hopes, trusts, and aspirations. He had taught the ploughman mathematics, but that ploughman had possessed in himself all the essential elements of the grandeur of the old prophets, glorified by the faith which the Son of Man did not find in the earth, but left behind him to grow in it, and which had grown to a noble growth of beauty and strength in this peasant, simple and patriarchal in the midst of a self-conceited age. And, oh! how good he had been to him! He had built a house that he might take him in from the cold, and make life pleasant to him, as in the presence of God. He had given him his heart every time he gave him his great manly hand. And this man, this friend, this presence of Christ, Hugh had forsaken, neglected, all but forgotten. He could not go, and, like the prodigal, fall down before him, and say, "Father, I have sinned against heaven and thee," for that heaven had taken him up out of his sight. He could only weep instead, and bitterly repent. Yes; there was one thing more he could do. Janet still lived. He would go to her, and confess his sin, and beg her forgiveness. Receiving it, he would be at peace. He knew David forgave him, whether he confessed or not; and that, if he were alive, David would seek his confession only as the casting away of the separation from his heart, as the banishment of the worldly spirit, and as the natural sign by which he might know that Hugh was one with him yet.

Janet was David's representative on earth: he would go to her.

So he returned, rich and great; rich in knowing that he was the child of Him to whom all the gold mines belong; and great in that humility which alone recognizes greatness, and in the beginnings of that meekness which shall inherit the earth. No more would he stunt his spiritual growth by self-satisfaction. No more would he lay aside, in the cellars of his mind, poor withered bulbs of opinions, which, but for the evil ministrations of that self-satisfaction, seeking to preserve them by drying and salting, might have been already bursting into blossoms of truth, of infinite loveliness.

He knew that Margaret thought far too well of him—honoured him greatly beyond his deserts. He would not allow her to be any longer thus deceived. He would tell her what a poor creature he was. But he would say too, that he hoped one day to be worthy of her praise, that he hoped to grow to what she thought him. If he should fail in convincing her, he would receive all the honour she gave him humbly, as paid, not to him, but to what he ought to be. God grant it might be as to his future self!

In this mood he went to Janet.

CHAPTER XXIV.

THE FIR-WOOD AGAIN.

Er stand vor der himmlischen Jungfrau. Da hob er den leichten, glänzenden Schleier, und—Rosenblüthchen sank in seine Arme.—NOVALIS.—*Die Lehrlinge zu Sais*

He stood before the heavenly Virgin (*Isis, the Goddess of Nature*). Then lifted he the light, shining veil, and—Rosebud (*his old love*) sank into his arms.

So womanly, so benigne, and so meek.
CHAUCER.—*Prol. to Leg. of Good Women.*

IT was with a mingling of strange emotions, that Hugh approached the scene of those not very old, and yet, to his feeling, quite early memories. The dusk was beginning to gather. The hoar-frost lay thick on the ground. The pine-trees stood up in the cold, looking, in their garment of spikes, as if the frost had made them. The rime on the gate was unfriendly, and chilled his hand. He turned into the foot-path. He saw the room David had built for him. Its thatch was one mass of mosses, whose colours were hidden now in the cuckoo-fruit of the frost. Alas! how Death had cast his deeper frost over all; for the man was gone from the hearth! But neither old Winter nor skeleton Death can withhold the feet of the little child Spring. She is stronger than both. Love shall conquer hate; and God will overcome sin.

He drew nigh to the door, trembling. It seemed strange to him that his nerves only, and not his mind, should feel.—In moments of unusual excitement, it sometimes happens that the only consciousness a strong man has of emotion, lies in an unwonted physical vibration, the mind itself refusing to be disturbed. It is, however, but a seeming: the emotion is so deep, that consciousness can lay hold of its physical result only.—The cottage looked the same as ever, only the peat-stack outside was smaller. In the shadowiness of the firs, the glimmer of a fire was just discernible on the kitchen window. He trembled so much that he could not enter. He would go into the fir-wood first, and see Margaret's tree, as he always called it in his thoughts and dreams.

Very poor and stunted and meagre looked the fir-trees of Turriepuffit, after the beeches and elms of Arnstead. The evening wind whistled keen and cold through their dry needles, and made them moan, as if because they were fettered, and must endure the winter in helpless patience. Here and there amongst them, rose the Titans of the little forest—the huge, old, contorted, wizard-like, yet benevolent beings—the Scotch firs. Towards one of these he bent his way. It was the one under which he had seen Margaret, when he met her first in the wood, with her whole soul lost in the waving of its wind-swung, sun-lighted top, floating about in the sea of air like a golden nest for some silvery bird of heaven. To think that the young girl to whom he had given the primrose he had just found, the then first-born of the spring, should now be the queen of his heart! Her childish dream of the angel haunting the wood had been true, only she was the angel herself. He drew near the place. How well he knew it! He seated himself, cold as it was in the February of Scotland, at the foot of the blessed tree. He did not know that it was cold.

While he sat with his eyes fixed on the ground, a light rustle in the fallen leaves made him raise them suddenly. It was all winter and fallen leaves about him; but he lifted his eyes, and in his soul it was summer: Margaret stood before him. He was not in the least surprised. For how can one wonder to see before his eyes, the form of which his soul is full?—there is no shock. She stood a little way off, looking—as if she wanted to be sure before she moved a step. She was dressed in a grey winsey gown, close to her throat and wrists. She had neither shawl nor bonnet. Her fine health kept her warm, even in a winter wood at sun-down. She looked just the same; —at home everywhere; most at home in Nature's secret chamber. Like the genius of the place, she made the winter-wood look homely. What were the oaks and beeches of Arnstead now? Homeliness and glory are Heaven.

She came nearer.

"Margaret!" he murmured, and would have risen.

"No, no; sit still," she rejoined, in a pleading tone. "I *thought* it was the angel in the picture. Now I know it. Sit still, dear Mr. Sutherland, one moment more."

Humbled by his sense of unworthiness, and a little distressed that she could so quietly reveal the depth of her feeling towards him, he said:

"Ah, Margaret! I wish you would not praise one so little deserving it."

"Praise?" she repeated, with an accent of wonder. "I praise you! No, Mr. Sutherland; that I am not guilty of. Next to my father, you made me know and feel. And as I walked here, I was thinking of the old times, and older times still; and all at once I saw the very picture out of the old Bible."

She came close to him now. He rose, trembling, but held out no hand, uttered no greeting.

"Margaret, dare I love you?" he faltered.

She looked at him with wide-open eyes.

"*Me?*" she said; and her eyes did not move from his. A slight rose-flush bloomed out on her motionless face.

"Will you be my wife?" he said, trembling yet more.

She made no answer, but looked at him still, with parted lips, motionless.

"I am very poor, Margaret. I could not marry now."

It was a stupid speech, but he made it.

"I don't care," she answered, with a voice like thinking, "if you never marry me."

He misunderstood her, and turned cold to the very heart. He misunderstood her stillness. Her heart lay so deep, that it took a long time for its feelings to reach and agitate the surface. He said no more, but turned away with a sigh.

"Come home to my mother," she said.

He obeyed mechanically, and walked in silence by her side. They reached the cottage and entered. Margaret said: "Here he is, mother;" and disappeared.

Janet was seated—in her widow's *mutch,* with the plain black ribbon down both sides, and round the back—in the arm-chair by the fire, pondering on the past, or gently dreaming of him that was gone. She turned her head. Sorrow had baptized her face with a new gentleness. The tender expression which had been but occasional while her husband lived, was almost constant now. She did not recognize Hugh. He saw it, and it added weight to his despair. He was left outside.

"Mother!" he said, involuntarily.

She started to her feet, cried: "My bairn! my bairn!" threw her arms around him, and laid her head on his bosom. Hugh sobbed as if his heart would break. Janet wept, but her weeping was quiet as a summer rain. He led her to her chair, knelt by her side, and hiding his face in her lap like a child, faltered out, interrupted by convulsive sobs:

"Forgive me; forgive me. I don't deserve it, but forgive me."

"Hoot awa! my bairn! my bonny man! Dinna greet that gait. The Lord preserve's! what are ye greetin' for? Are na ye come hame to yer ain? Didna Dawvid aye say—'Gie the lad time, woman. It's unco chaip, for the Lord's aye makin't. The best things is aye the maist plentifu'. Gie the lad time, my bonny woman!'—didna he say that? Ay, he ca'd me his bonny woman, ill as I deserved it at his han'. An' it's no for me to say ae word agen you, Maister Sutherlan', gin ye had been a hantle waur nor a young thochtless lad cudna weel help bein'. An' noo ye're come hame, an' nothing cud glaidden my heart mair, 'cep', maybe, the Maister himsel' was to say to my man: 'Dawvid! come furth."

Hugh could make no reply. He got hold

of Margaret's creepie, which stood in its usual place, and sat down upon it, at the old woman's feet. She gazed in his face for a while, and then, putting her arm round his neck, drew his head to her bosom, and fondled him as if he had been her own first-born.

"But eh! yer bonnie face is sharp an' sma' to what it used to be, Maister Sutherlan'. I doot ye hae come through a heap o' trouble."

"I'll tell you all about it," said Hugh.

"Na, na; bide still a wee. I ken a' aboot it frae Maggy. An' guid preserve's! ye're clean perished wi' cauld. Lat me up, my bairn."

Janet rose, and made up the fire, which soon cast a joyful glow throughout the room. The peat-fire in the little cottage was a good symbol of the heart of its mistress: it gave far more heat than light. And for my part, dear as light is, I like heat better. She then put on the kettle,—or the *boiler* I think she called it—saying:

"I'm jist gaein' to mak' ye a cup o' tay, Mr. Sutherlan'. It's the handiest thing, ye ken.

An' I doot ye're muckle in want o' something. Wad ye no tak' a drappy oot o' the bottle, i' the mane time?"

"No, thank you," said Hugh, who longed to be alone, for his heart was cold as ice; "I would rather wait for the tea; but I should be glad to have a good wash, after my journey."

"Come yer wa's, than, ben the hoose. I'll jist gang an' get a drappy o' het water in a decanter. Bide ye still by the fire."

Hugh stood, and gazed into the peat-fire. But he saw nothing in it. A light step passed him several times, but he did not heed it. The loveliest eyes looked earnestly towards him as they passed, but his were not lifted to meet their gaze.

"Noo, Maister Sutherlan', come this way."

Hugh was left alone at length, in the room where David had slept, where David had used to pray. He fell on his knees, and rose comforted by the will of God. A few things of Margaret's were about the room. The dress he had seen her in at Mrs. Elton's, was hanging by the bed. He kissed the folds of the garment, and said: "God's will be done." He had just finished a hasty ablution when Janet called him.

"Come awa', Maister Sutherlan'; come ben to yer ain chaumer," said she, leading the way to the room she still called *the study*. Margaret was there. The room was just as he had left it. A bright fire was on the hearth. Tea was on the table, with eggs, and oatcakes, and *flour-scons* in abundance; for Janet had the best she could get for Margaret, who was only her guest for a little while. But Hugh could not eat. Janet looked distressed, and Margaret glanced at him uneasily.

"Do eat something, Mr. Sutherland," said Margaret.

Hugh looked at her involuntarily. She did not understand his look, and it alarmed her. His countenance was changed.

"What is the matter, dear —— Hugh?" she said, rising, and laying her hand on his shoulder.

"Hoots! lassie," broke in her mother; "are

ye makin' love till a man, a *gentleman*, afore my verra een?"

"He did it first, mother," answered Margaret, with a smile.

A pang of hope shot through Hugh's heart.

"Ow! that's the gait o't, is't? The bairn's gane dementit! Ye're no efter merryin' a gentleman, Maggy? Na, na, lass!"

So saying, the old lady, rather crossly, and very imprudently, left the room to fill the teapot in the kitchen.

"Do you remember this?" said Margaret,—who felt that Hugh must have misunderstood something or other,—taking from her pocket a little book, and from the book a withered flower.

Hugh saw that it was like a primrose, and hoped against hope that it was the one which he had given to her, on the spring morning in the fir-wood. Still, a feeling very different from his might have made her preserve it. He *must* know all about it.

"Why did you keep that?" he said.

"Because I loved you."

"Loved me?"

"Yes. Didn't you know?"

"Why did you say, then, that you didn't care if—if—?"

"Because love is enough, Hugh.—That was why."

THE END.

CPSIA information can be obtained
at www.ICGtesting.com
Printed in the USA
LVHW100431110522
718424LV00003B/109

9 783375 006334